Sarah Dunant is a writer and broa
work included presenting BBC2's
gramme, *The Late Show*, for a nun
editor of *The War of the Words*, a collection of essays on political correctness, and seven novels including *Snow Storms in a Hot Climate* and *Transgressions*.

Roy Porter is professor in the social history of medicine at the Wellcome Institute for the History of Medicine. He is currently working on a general history of medicine, on a history of the Bethlem Hospital and on the Enlightenment in Britain. Recent books include *Doctor of Society: Thomas Beddoes and the Sick Trade in Late Enlightenment England* and *London: A Social History*.

The Age of Anxiety

Edited by
Sarah Dunant
and
Roy Porter

A *Virago* Book

Published by Virago Press 1997

First published by Virago Press 1996

A CIP catalogue record for this book
is available from the British Library

ISBN 1 86049 308 4

Typeset in Ehrhardt by M Rules
Printed and bound in Great Britain by
Clays Ltd, St Ives plc

Virago
A Division of
Little, Brown and Company (UK)
Brettenham House
Lancaster Place
London WC2E 7EN

Contents

Acknowledgements

Anxieties, by definition, are as much in the mind as in reality. Confronting and analysing them, especially at this particular moment in history, was bound to be a challenge. It is a challenge that every one of the ten essayists in this book has risen to with grace, intellectual vision and fortitude. For that, and for their patience and forbearance during discussions and occasional rewrites, the editors are both admiring and grateful. A similar debt is owed to Lennie Goodings at Virago, without whom we would all have been even more anxious . . .

Introducing Anxiety

> The world was full of omens of its own destruction. New plagues swept across the globe: people died in agony, some shrivelled to skeletons, some pouring blood and fluids from every orifice. Children began to wheeze and choke on the very air they breathed. A heart of a pig was found to beat in the body of a man. There were floods where there had been droughts and drought where there had been water. And in a city in the west a woman who had lain as if dead for many months was found to be with child.

AIDS, Eboli, asthma from pollution, scientific research, global warming and a freak story of rape from a New York hospital. It doesn't take a lot to whip up a dark-ages-type millennial fever. For the end of the twentieth century read the end of the tenth and the French monk, Adémar:

> In these times a terrible plague was sent by divine command across the western people. There appeared signs of harmful droughts, excessive rains, numerous eclipses of sun and moon . . . terrible famines, so that innumerable common folks were killed and a brother killed his own sister and ate her.

Of course we are more sophisticated now. We understand that the year 2000 is just that – another date on the calendar – and one which, given its sense of occasion, allows us a unique opportunity to take stock of ourselves. We expect such occasions to cause us a modicum of anxiety. (Interestingly, the word itself didn't exist when Adémar was writing, though the feeling it describes – 'being troubled in mind about an uncertain event' – obviously did.) But do we really handle it any better?

In certain key ways millennial anxieties have changed less than one might think from the year 1000 to 2000. Floods, droughts, plagues, the keen sense of nature out of kilter is as much a familiar motif of anxiety to us now as it was to people then. The difference is that while they saw natural disasters as God's way of drawing attention to man's evil, we see it more as man's chronic mismanagement of nature. God – unless you happen to be an American fundamentalist – has nothing to do with it.

Evil, however, appears to be making something of a come back. While we may no longer talk about the wrath of God, when faced with events like the Bulger killing, the West murders and the massacre at Dunblane, commentators increasingly reach for the word evil. It covers, of course, a multitude of anxieties. By default it explains the inexplicable, it offers more reassurance than the idea of random horror and it excuses us from deeper attempts at understanding. It also reflects our growing sense of helplessness.

That is something else we share with the end of the tenth century: a mounting panic about how – if at all – we can rectify the damage. When it was a simple contest between God and the Devil there was at least a strategy of repentance. The Middle Ages could resort to sackcloth and ashes and mobilise armies of flagellants to show God they meant business. Now such a display would probably be seen as further evidence of S-and-M decadence in a post-liberation culture. And liberalism, as we shall see, is already taking the rap for a lot of millennial uncertainties.

Our sense of powerlessness is not limited to the environment or acts of random violence. For many people in the western world the unprecedented expansion of everything from technology through communication to shopping has brought with it not only increased demands of choice (in itself something of an anxiety) but also an expanding potential for feeling out of control.

As Paul Kennedy illustrated in his book, *Towards a 21st Century*, a world economy ever more concentrated into fewer hands and complemented by national governments with an eye firmly on the next election and short-term popularity, makes for cynical politics and undermines any real attempt at radical change. (We may all know that car pollution leads to asthma in our kids, but who is really going to be brave enough to take drastic steps to do something about it? For car pollution read the first BSE scare of the late eighties when it was less politically damaging to mop up and cover up rather than face the consequences. In both cases the problems are/were too great and the solutions too complex for us to contemplate until it was too late.) And the more we despise politicians for not biting the bullet, the more we are really despising ourselves for not being able to take control.

This lack of control has leaked into our personal lives, too. As global capitalism defines the need for shifting labour patterns and structural unemployment, the job security which was once the bedrock of the working population has now been effectively eroded. Education, which used to be the ladder to an upwardly mobile future, is now, as often as not, simply the gateway to the dole queue. Instead of having one skill you are now expected to have two or three: portfolio lives may sound desirable on paper but how you go about getting one makes for its own sense of uncertainty. With life expectancy growing thanks to medical science and technology and a predicted fall in the birth rate, we are all increasingly worried about how we shall support ourselves into old age. Given the demographics of the baby boomers, that 'we' contains a large number of people hitting middle age at the same time as the turn of the century – a certain recipe for exaggerated anxiety.

Of course some of this is peculiar to Britain. A country which fifty years ago re-invented itself as a welfare state, and has spent the last twenty years divesting itself of the notion of both state and welfare, is bound to provoke anxieties in the free-milk generation that grew up with it and now has to cope with change. But there is evidence that it is not just the over-forties who are feeling it. The last essay in this book comes from a seventeen-year-old who will be twenty-one in the year 2000. Bidisha Bandyopadhyay may have more energy and flexibility than her elders, but she also exhibits an almost pragmatic pessimism when it comes to what is achievable and what isn't.

For many, the future now seems less about going forwards than going backwards. A recent Mori poll revealed that over 50 per cent of people living in Britain believe that things are getting worse. Mix the insecurity of global economics with the threat of family breakdown and increased fear of crime, violence and racial tension and you have a population which feels it difficult to handle today, let alone contemplate tomorrow. And tomorrow, when it comes to a new millennium, is an intimidatingly big sheet of blank paper.

How far these fears and anxieties about violence, the family, crime, technology, race, etc. are justified, and how far they are by-products of a society in change, exacerbated by a state of the art media flirting with millennial fever, is something that each of the essays in the volume seeks to address. But underneath their arguments certain constants emerge.

The first is to do with our notion of progress.

For the last couple of hundred years we have been hitting the ends of centuries with a balance sheet that was recognisably more positive than negative. Before the prophets of progress and the Enlightenment there had been little enthusiasm for the idea of a real *future*; hitherto all imagined Utopias had been set in the past or were other-worldly (heaven itself). But looking back on the big double zero of 1800, William Hazlitt could write 'a new world was opening to the astonished sight . . . Scenes, lovely as hope can paint, dawned on the imagination; visions of unsullied bliss lulled the senses, nothing was too mighty for the new begotten hope.'

Much of this optimism was connected with the American and French revolutions, which offered a Promethean sense of man finally in control of his own destiny, destroying old empires and regimes and – in the case of France – instituting a new order so ripe with possibility that it even had its own new calendar commencing with *An* I.

By the time the century actually turned (*An* IX), the joy of the revolution had already curdled into the Terror, and the emergence of a leader who was to bring war and carnage to Europe for the next fifteen years. Nevertheless, 1800 in philosophic terms signalled the replacement of Time's cycle by Time's arrow, and the notion that the future would be better than the past, thanks to reason and science and industry and technology.

Our own century opened with a similar balance sheet. Yes, there were examples of moral panic at what is now defined as *fin de siècle* decadence; the world of bohemian Paris and Vienna, of Rimbaud and Wilde; art repudiating bourgeois morality for drink and drugs, strange sex and the belief that true artistic creativity could only come out of corruption. There was tremendous anxiety over syphilis and fears of degeneration. (Every end of century needs its plague fears, of course. For syphilis now read AIDS, and for AIDS read Oscar Moore's defiant personal journey through contemporary plague anxiety.)

But the chorus of voices which met the twentieth century were far from uniformly critical. They also included scientists and visionaries who saw a Brave New World ahead without recognising the irony in that quotation. Alfred Russel Wallace, co-founder with Darwin of Evolutionism, welcomed the new century with a volume extolling Victorian progress and anticipating even better times to come. There was enormous enthusiasm and optimism for the control over nature that science would bring. Marxism offered a dream of a more just society and in the very year of 1900 the young Sigmund Freud published *The Interpretation of Dreams*, uncovering the notion of the psyche, and thereby giving people the prospect of understanding their inner selves and so more effectively controlling their own destinies.

The rest, as they say, is history. As we all know only too well, the century that brought us electric light, air travel, antibiotics and a million other advances also brought us the bomb, two devastating world wars, the mechanisation of genocide, an unprecedented displacement of humanity over the globe and an orgy of torture and state violence. For perfectibility read corruptibility, for belief in progress read naiveté. When the definitive history of the twentieth century comes to be written (and as the historian Eric Hobsbawm says in his magnificent *The Age of Extremes*, it is impossible to do that when one is still living it), we may find that we can be kinder to ourselves. But the reality remains that as we enter the twenty-first century the idea that future equals progress has sustained a philosophic body blow from which it will not easily recover.

What also emerges from many of these essays is the place of sixties liberalism within this century's disillusionment with progress. Some of this, of course, is just party politics. 'Isms' often find themselves at war with one another, and it was inevitable that Thatcherism (and Reaganism) would condemn a left-of-centre ideology committed to exploring sexual and emotional freedom and challenging accepted codes of behaviour and establishment values. (Interestingly, Thatcherism had no trouble in condoning the equivalent within the economic sphere, but then that, it would claim, was about creation of wealth and therefore the ultimate public good.)

Despite the manifest disorder in the ranks of the right, sixties-bashing is still a familiar riff in the music of modern British politics (even New Labour seem to suffer from collective memory loss when it comes to sex'n drugs and rock'n roll). But underneath the political point-scoring there are serious issues to be addressed, about the kind of society we want to live in and how it is policed, both literally and covertly. The current moral panic over levels of violence, crime and family breakdown may seek to lay much of the blame at the feet of sixties liberals, but the truth, as a number of the essays in this book show, is both more complex and more exacting. Voices like those of Linda Grant on violence, Michael Neve on the family and Susie Orbach on a future for psychoanalysis refuse to follow the liberal-bashing line, but take a more challenging approach in dissecting the meanings behind the anxieties.

In many of these essays different roads lead to the same question. As our choices appear to expand and our sense of control appears to diminish, how do we stop ourselves from being frightened of the future? As a medical broadcaster, Geoff Watts spends his life keeping abreast of an almost constant series of minor medical and scientific revolutions. If *he* feels overwhelmed by them, what hope for the likes of the rest of us? Yet his optimism, like his ability to communicate it, remains unquenched, drawing attention to the importance of the way the media can alleviate, explore or pander to our sense of panic. Geoff Mulgan, as director of the think-tank Demos, is able both to revel in the freedoms of the new technology while also keeping an acute balance sheet on the gains and losses when it comes to a sense of control. But it's absolutely clear from his essay that there's no going back, and that we would be foolish to want to do so. For all of us teetering on the edge of a new millennium this, of course, is the trick: to learn how to embrace the explosion of new possibilities while still preserving a sense of identity and belonging. The fact that 'community' is the new buzz-word of the decade shows how vital that anxiety has become. Belonging is the subject of Michael Ignatieff's essay, with its analysis of how, in a modern world, we can square the old circle of freedom versus responsibilities, civic duties versus individual rights.

Not all the essayists in this book are optimistic about life past the millennium. But they all – to quote Hemingway – think that the world is a place worth fighting for. The question is how best to mount the battle. Some of the weapons might come from the future itself. At a time of growing disillusionment with politics and suspicion of media empires, many believe that the Internet has the potential to offer a radical alternative; creating a world-wide community of like-minded people swapping ideas and information and setting their own agendas for pressure, protest or change. (Witness how the Singapore government set about censoring the local Internet when it began a bulletin board voicing criticisms of the state, or how quickly, when the French started nuclear testing in the south Pacific in 1995, the idea of boycotting French goods spread across continents through the Internet – from small keystrokes whole vineyards can be threatened.)

Other weapons will be more traditional. All societies need some kind of inspirational vision of the future to sustain them. On the cusp of a millennium, that need is all the greater. Where politics and economics are found wanting, culture, both in terms of art and ideas, can at least offer imaginative alternatives. Both the poet and novelist Fred D'Aguiar and the philosopher Mary Midgley combat anxiety with vision. As a British Caribbean writer, D'Aguiar's focus is race; his essay a meditation on how we might come to compose the last novel, poem or song about slavery, how through writing, reshaping, re-creating a historical pain, we might be able to absorb, digest and move on from the legacy of it. Midgley's canvas is the environment. A philosopher who has lived through most of the century she now writes about, she takes off where this introduction began, analysing our increasing sense of helplessness at the environmental crisis we have created around us. For her, the success of any vision is dependent on how we ourselves cope with the anxiety. She defines anxiety less as a continual state of worry and more as an excess of frustrated energy: turned in on itself it engenders a form of paralysis, but directed outwards it can be both a release and a way of mobilising us into action.

A thousand years on, even without God's wrath to terrorise us, we shall probably not embrace this new millennium with the same transcendental joy that, say, Wordsworth embraced the turn of his century. We might not feel that it is bliss to be alive in this dawn or even (as our youngest contributor can testify) very heaven to be young. On the other hand, we have come a long way in 1000 years. Whatever plans you might have for a millennial party, they don't need to include this: 'Go in, pass the night in sackcloth, sanctify a fast, call a solemn assembly, gather all the elders and inhabitants of the land . . . and cry to the Lord.'

Better to sit at home and read the collected works of Woody Allen. Now there's a late-twentieth-century man who knows what to do with his anxiety:

> More than any time in history, mankind faces a crossroad. One path leads to despair and utter hopelessness, the other to total extinction. Let us pray that we have the wisdom to choose correctly.

Sarah Dunant and Roy Porter
London, April 1996

The Age of Anxiety

Geoff Mulgan

High Tech and High Angst

Not long ago the things that frightened us most were gods and natural disasters, dragons and demons. But it is a characteristic of modern times that we have now transferred those fears to our own creations. The most potent sources of fear today are nearly all either technologies or the direct results of technology: nuclear weapons and power stations, vicious new designer viruses and microscopic surveillance bugs. Many of these are directly life-threatening. But strangely it is a more benign technology, the computer, which has probably done even more to stoke anxieties. Although the computer is ubiquitous, embedded in wristwatches and washing machines, car engines and lifts, there are very few distopian fears that have not been projected on to it.

Some have foreseen human obsolescence, and ever since the 1950s it has been common to warn that computers would destroy millions of jobs. More recently President Mitterand's former adviser, Jacques Attali, and Jeremy

Rifkin have written of a proletariat that has been given its marching orders, displaced by machines. Others have seen computers as the enemies of liberty, likely to usher in a new era of totalitarian control, with government databases achieving the clinical efficiency that Hitler and Stalin never managed.

In the era of expert systems, smart cards and closed circuit TV cameras in high streets, such anxieties seem to be reaching a new fever pitch. The media are full of lurid tales of computer viruses that could bring down the world's financial system, hackers or terrorists taking control of nuclear weapons systems, and pornographers using the Internet or CD-ROMs to direct hard-core pornography into school classrooms. Popular culture now invariably situates information technology in downbeat, insecure futures dominated by monstrous global corporations: the doomed androids of *Blade Runner*, the decaying anarchy of cyberspace in the cyberpunk literature, worlds where no one is in control any more.

One of the odd features of these anxieties is that the increasingly febrile promotion of computers, not least by the world's pre-eminent informational billionaire Bill Gates, seems to be both amplifying and mirroring the spread of new fears. There is something suspicious about the sheer utopian certainty of the generally young, affluent and still predominantly male computer nuts. Books like supersalesman Nicholas Negroponte's *Being Digital* and magazines like *Wired* emphatically assert the historical inevitability of a world dominated by computers. Their assertions are all the more disturbing because they appear to have no historical sense, no appreciation that during the twentieth century naive optimism about technology has been comprehensively qualified by the experiences of everything from the atom bomb to food additives. After twenty-five years, when computers have brought neither heaven nor hell, the vehemence of the optimists – still pushing the same arguments that first took shape in the 1960s – engenders legitimate suspicion.

Yet the claims of both the optimists and the pessimists tend to be misplaced. We seem to be reliving that now familiar cycle whereby a new technology is greeted with horror, then accepted as normal and finally dressed in its own nostalgic hue (think for example of the steam engine). The real likelihood is that the Internet will be neither the most wonderful medium ever invented nor the enemy of a common culture, just as the computer has already turned out to be neither a great liberator, with the capacity to break down all hierarchies, nor a sinister ally of the powers that be.

Scratch beneath the surface of the standard arguments and you soon find other hopes and fears. Often, too, you find that what is really at issue is a shifting balance of power. You can see some of this in the jobs market. Technologies have always created and destroyed jobs, empowered some relative to others. But what has changed recently is that whereas for a long time it was assumed that the main victims of technology would be relatively unskilled workers in manufacturing, today job losses have spread far beyond factories and back offices to touch the most prestigious professions. Today's main victims of technology are not only the thousands of bank tellers and shop assistants but also layers of middle management whose role as conduits for information up and down organisational hierarchies has become redundant. Professors find that their students, by borrowing a video, can access a rather better lecture than the one they've been delivering for years. Lawyers find themselves faced by advertisements offering online services giving legal information at a fraction of the price they charge. Doctors' monopoly of knowledge is threatened by diagnostic databases with which, at least in principle, patients could interpret their symptoms more reliably than overstressed medicos. Writers used to the days of the typewriter and the pen feel threatened by a culture in which everything can be endlessly changed, rewritten and overwritten, and where authorship is ever less tangible. And as always in such cases, the losers can see what they are losing more clearly than the winners can see their gains.

Within the workplace, power is shifting not so much to people with a formal qualification but rather to those with some special capacity to judge, or to sift knowledge, that cannot be easily replicated by machines. This is why the pay for star performers in corporate law, the arts, consultancy and medicine has risen so much higher above the average. It is also, intriguingly, why one of the main increases in jobs is in areas that have no technological element, the face-to-face tasks of care or personal services, ranging from residential homes to prostitution, counselling to therapy.

These shifts in the balance of work, away from the old hierarchies of both manual and mental labour, are bound to be disorienting. The same is true for many who work from home; teleworkers who have had to turn bedrooms into offices out of necessity rather than choice have found it not only lonely but also unreliable. Nor is it easy to accept a world of work where function and place have been separated in so many other ways: how many people reserving rooms at Best Western hotels in the USA would feel comfortable if they knew that their reservations were being taken by inmates of the Arizona Women's Penitentiary?

But our current worries aren't simply the inevitable consequences of change. I think there may also be a more subtle source of anxiety at work as well, a less obvious shift in mentalities. To see this we need first to understand why information and information technology seem to make us powerful, and more certain. In principle, the growth of information and knowledge which has become almost exponential both in the natural sciences and in terms of the formal production of words, bits and images should make it easier for us to map all the things that may affect us and thus make us more certain, more secure and more in control. The great claim of an era of rational enquiry is that it puts paid to the uncertainties of superstition, when our lives and world seemed surrounded by incomprehensible and impenetrable forces. By contrast in an age of plentiful information, every question becomes answerable. If you don't know the answer, you can reach an expert who does, or search through an interactive CD-ROM to seek it out. Personal information too becomes transparent, all the way from credit card details to genetic predispositions.

The great promise of technology, in other words, is that it dispels anxiety and uncertainty. The computer gives this idea its purest expression. It is not coincidental that ideas of control were central to the early theorists of computing. The American scientist Norbert Wiener coined the term 'cybernetics', drawing on the Greek word for a helmsman, to define a science of control and feedback: a systematic science which could be applied to everything from anti-aircraft guns (the first topic he worked on) to the management of organisations, battles or factories. In cybernetics, communication channels pass on not only the commands but also the feedback on how the commands are being carried out and how the wider environment is responding. They return us to the original meaning of control, which derives from the Latin *'contra rotulare'*, the practice of comparing something against the rolls.

This promise of control remains paramount. For most managers spending millions on a new computer system, the attraction is to be able to know in real time who is spending what, which machines are working, which products are selling. For generals, the appeal of the 'twenty-four hour battle ground', and of the systems of communication, command and control and intelligence (3 CI as it is called in the jargon) is that they seem to dispel the typically blind chaos of war. For the fourteen-year-old playing on a console in his room, the promise of being in complete control of a game, without having to worry about team mates, friends or girls, is obvious too.

And yet the great paradox of the information age is that it has brought not greater knowledge, certainty and wisdom, but probably less. There is scarcely a field where more information has, once and for all, made things more controllable. Instead, the characteristic feature of the information age is an explosion of options, an explosion of counter strategies, of facts which cannot be wholly trusted, of complexities that become not clearer, even if they are more visible. And because the explosion of IT means that ever more of our knowledge is not first hand, not derived directly from our own senses, our confidence in it is necessarily always qualified.

In other words we gain control and lose it simultaneously. When Kevin Kelly, the editor of *Wired*, cheerleading magazine of the computer culture, wrote his definitive and highly entertaining book on the world emerging from the computer revolution, he called it *Out of Control*. In it he argued that the sheer quantity of interconnected systems now operating in the global network means that no one can exercise control as though in a closed system. Instead, the old way of thinking of lives, societies and economies as mechanical systems, subject to predictable regularities, and under the control of institutions with clearly visible levers, has become obsolete. The informational world, according to Kelly, mirrors life, a natural, living system. This may be deeply traumatic for people brought up with the idea that there is a supreme authority, whether that of a god, or a monarchy, or their political descendants who invested in the state and political agents a similar capacity to control societies and deliver either good or evil. But it is the reality we now have to live with.

There is, of course, a benign side to this lack of control. It is precisely the 'out of control' character of the system which encourages libertarians to praise the Internet and the computer as agents of liberation. Everyone can become their own publisher; everyone can copy and disseminate information without having to win a licence from the government or strike a deal with big shopping chains.

And, according to the conventional wisdom, every attempt by governments to restrict the flow of information has become futile. In the 1970s the Shah of Iran was unable to insulate his subjects from gaining access to smuggled cassette tapes of the speeches of the Ayatollah Khomeini, and throughout the Cold War the old Soviet authorities found it hard to jam all the signals from the Voice of America or the BBC. In the same way today no government can block the television programmes signalled down on them by geostationary satellites, or block the flow of data on undersea fibre optic cables. Information as a whole is achieving the freedoms that the press won in the great struggles of the renaissance, when Milton's *Areopagitica* and later the US Constitution's First Amendment crystallised the idea that governments should no longer have power over communication, the power to license information providers.

Such is the standard view. At the moment it is being fiercely contested by national governments. Fascinating battles are currently under way over just how far governments can control their own informational space. Singapore is a particularly good example, because it is both one of the world's most technologically advanced nations and one with a peculiarly controlling and authoritarian government. To keep disturbing messages out, its government has long prohibited domestic satellite dishes, as well as banning access to certain Internet sites, although smart users can still access these via a different server based in another country. The government has also cleverly mobilised its own citizens to swamp critical bulletin boards with loyal Singaporean responses. In Singapore, its main aim has been to maintain a restrictive political and social order. But elsewhere in the world similar policies have arisen from public pressure to protect children. The German government, along with a number of US states, has tried to restrict access to pornography on the Internet, holding the big servers like Compuserve responsible for the services they carry, and the US government's latest telecommunications legislation has prohibited pornography on the net.

Although it is impossible to regulate contents on a system as vast and diverse as the Internet (it would be rather like trying to regulate what people say in telephone conversations), in practice these battles are far less one-sided than the technological libertarians assumed. As the Burmese government showed with its successful exclusion of television cameras during the struggles of the late 1980s, it is still possible to control the terms of access to the world's information society, at least on the major channels.

What all these governments are trying to do is to preserve simplicity. Within each society there are minorities wanting access to new kinds of information – it may be news about the peccadilloes of government ministers, or kinky sex chat lines. Access to information magnifies the power and number of these minorities; restricting it perpetuates the fiction of uniformity. Governments are also trying to foster an idea of childhood as a protected domain: protected not only from pornography and extreme violence but also from overmanipulative advertising messages. Each step they take to contain new technologies can be bypassed by the next technology. Even though governments are still able to meet parents' demands for them to protect most of their children most of the time, at the edges, control is probably impossible. Paradoxically, the experience of governments in trying to keep up with a rapidly evolving technology mirrors that of citizens who experience a continual race simply to stand still. Take even the simplest activity, something like buying food. Information systems have made it possible dramatically to improve the distribution and management of food. Supermarkets can stock exotic fruit like Rambutans, Star Fruit and Durians, with immediate feedback on which ones are being bought. Consumers can in principle use databases to find out far more information about the effects of each fruit on their health: the risks of different types of cancer or heart disease, novel recipes for using them, even perhaps some literary references. All of this makes our choices more informed. But it demands of us a major investment of time and psychic energy, and the strange thing that happens as you come closer to increasing quantities of information is that you often feel more aware of what you don't know rather than more confident about what you do.

Food may seem a banal example, but precisely the same factors apply to any organisation. More information means more choices, more awareness of the relative standing of each information source, more variables, more complexities – and all ultimately coming into human minds that find it difficult to cope with this level of bombardment.

But it is not just the gap between the volume of information and the poor processing power of the human brain, and the gap between the desire for control and the difficulty in achieving it, that explain our anxiety. I think there may be a deeper reason. The pioneers of computing, and particularly Claude Shannon, the definer of communication theory, had an insight about the fundamental nature of information which is instructive. They argued that what distinguishes real information from non-information is its improbability. If we know what the next word of a sentence is going to be, that word doesn't provide us with any information. If we know exactly what is going to happen on the next page of a book, it is not providing us with anything new and tangible. In financial markets, the greatest value of a piece of information is not when it tells you that a share price has moved by one point, but when it tells you that the price has jumped, or is about to jump. The greatest value of a piece of gossip is the discovery of an unexpected affair, not a predictable one.

So information gives us new facts from among a range of options of varying degrees of improbability. It is, as Gregory Bateson put it, a difference that makes another difference, and the more improbable the new piece of information, the more informing it is. This notion may seem rather abstract. But it did make it possible to model information mathematically, and show how much information a communications channel could carry.

This idea of improbability helps us to understand the nature of information more generally. The fascinating thing about an explosion of information is that it is also an explosion of improbability. Sure, most advertisements are predictable, most conversations have more to do with passing the time than with conveying knowledge. But far more information means, paradoxically, a far less comprehensible environment and an exponential growth of theoretical possibilities. This is obviously true in specific fields. The explosion of scientific knowledge means that there are many more areas where unpredictable advances are now possible, or likely. It also means that science has moved far beyond the capacity of any one person to grasp. In culture, it will become far harder (though perhaps also far more attractive) to construct stable 'canons' within fixed national cultures when the sheer volume of literature, film or music is mushrooming. In daily life it means that even simple decisions have to be chosen from a range of different possibilities rather than simply assumed.

There are several possible responses. One is simply to retreat to simplicity, to seek out a straightforward and uncluttered life. Among modern politicians, a hero is Thomas Jefferson who took pride in never reading newspapers while he was running for president of the USA. We should expect an information-rich society also to be one with far more retreats, far more specialised forms of seclusion and tranquillity, and far more philosophies proclaiming the virtues of simple lives of purity and integrity. Indeed in North America there are already burgeoning groups proclaiming the virtues of simpler, less stressed lives, and getting rid of the information technology seems to be key to this.

A second option is to use technology itself to solve the problem. Huge amounts of money are now being invested to devise programs that reduce the daunting complexity and choice that the information explosion is bringing. The goal is to find programs that will make it possible for computers to sift and select from near-infinite quantities of information, fitting their choices to what they know about our own tastes and interests and, as far as possible, also allowing at least for that element of randomness, of browsing and roaming that we also seem to need.

A third option is to use technologies to release more time for us to spend making our choices. One version of this story was told by Isaac Asimov, who used it to explain why he was the most important individual who had ever lived. The story went like this. In the 1940s Asimov started writing novels about robots and computers. In these books he thought through some of the issues and problems that would arise from artificial forms of intelligence, the ethical problems that would be faced as humans tried to protect themselves from potentially hostile robots. His books were avidly read by scientists who then went on to experiment with the very earliest thinking computers – first, crude ones to break codes or work out pi to the millionth decimal point, later, ones that could play chess and, finally, more complex machines that could recognise patterns like voices, fingerprints or even human faces. Gradually fiction turned into fact, and robots began to appear on factory floors, at shopping tills or in garages doing MOT tests.

Of course, when robots appeared in daily life, they didn't look like human beings or the R2D2 of *Star Wars*. Instead, they appeared as disembodied limbs spraying car doors or moving goods around warehouses. But the important point was that in each case they were used to replace boring repetitive toil. This is the key to why computers not only create greater uncertainty but also liberate us to use our capacities better to cope with it. For most of our existence as a species humans lived as gatherers and hunters, roaming in small bands, and using much of their intelligence and all of their senses to survive. Then, when 5,000–10,000 years ago population pressures led us to settle and become agriculturalists, we found ourselves condemned to backbreaking and repetitive work, sowing, ploughing and reaping, and working far longer hours. Two hundred years ago the industrial revolution took this a stage further, making children work fourteen-hour days in factory jobs that used only a minuscule proportion of their intelligence, subordinating all life to the needs of industry.

According to this story, IT, prompted by the fictions of Asimov, becomes the *deus ex machina*, the liberator that can return us to meaningful lives by taking on all of these dull repetitive tasks, enabling us to concentrate on the thinking or caring jobs that we do best, preferably for the sixteen hours that comprised the normal working week in prehistoric times. For a time we may find this transition disorienting because it makes us again masters of our own destiny. But before too long we will be able to liberate our intelligence to cope with exploding information and choices, no longer delegating our decisions to supermarket managers or politicians.

So much for the fairy story. Isaac Asimov's claim to historical significance is weak. Scientists like Alan Turing,

Vannerar Bushe and Norbert Wiener were well on their way without having to read his books. But like all fairy stories it has a grain of truth, and not simply because it signals the importance of fiction as a source for science. The computer may not be a liberator for everyone. But it does represent a step change in the place of human intelligence – extending it in the way that binoculars, a camera, or microscope extend the eyes, and mechanics extend the muscles. If it really can master information and make it invisible, reduce the choices and anxieties, then for most people it may indeed liberate time for other things rather than giving us even more to worry about. So far it remains unclear whether this is possible. Working hours have started rising again after a century of decline, partly because of declining competitiveness in the west and partly because women's massive entry into the labour market has so sharply heightened competition for jobs. But in principle the goal of using technology to further liberate us from unnecessary work remains valid.

There is also another reason for hoping that the current wave of informational anxieties may be transitional: a generational one. If you search very carefully you can find an invisible line cutting through the middle of most western societies. It's a bit like the line that once divided people who had experienced the First World War from those who hadn't. On one side of this new line are the people brought up before computers became part of everyday life. On the other side are the generations for whom computers are becoming unexceptionable: part of the fabric of games and schools, the normal means for sending messages, doing your maths or making music; tools with many virtues and vices, but hardly to be feared.

In terms of dates of birth, the cut-off comes around

1965 – roughly four years before the cinema gave us one of the definitive visions of the computer as the enemy, and successor, of humanity in the form of HAL in Stanley Kubrick's *2001*.

Since I was born just before this, I'm a member of the last generation not to be brought up with computers. I began to use them only in my twenties – initially to program synthesisers and drum machines, and to write using crude word-processing packages. When I was a small child, I had to make do with toy trains and Ladybird books and a dog-eared 1913 edition of the *Encyclopaedia Britannica*. Multimedia CD-ROMs and Sega would have seemed like science fiction.

This generational shift means that we are now in a long transition. At the moment we have fifty years of pre-computer cohorts who will live and die, most of them never quite at ease with the new machines (and often writing bitter diatribes about how computers will destroy culture or democracy or community). Only around 2010 or even 2020 will we see the first generation of leaders for whom computers are more familiar than cows or sheep, more ubiquitous than coins, a generation who will probably have spent as much time communicating with machines as with people.

It is worth resting for a moment on this, because it is easy to get caught up in shorter time horizons of optimism and fear, scares and hype. Information technologies have been good at encouraging hysterical short-termism. Successive inventions such as the first Apple Macs, Minitel, Windows 95 and Netscape softwares have spawned bubbles of excitement and excess. In response, there has been no shortage of commentators – all of them, of course, born long before 1965 – warning either that computers and multimedia will bring slavery and misery or that they are banal; a new way of getting your local grocer to deliver to the home, a new version of the encyclopaedia or the video store, but nothing remotely resembling a revolution.

These kneejerk responses are misleading. One of the consistent features of the truly important, transforming technologies is that they take a very long time to shape life. Their rhythms are far slower than those of particular decades or business cycles. Electricity for example took at least seventy years to make its full impact, reshaping not only the home with dozens of domestic appliances like Hoovers and washing machines, TV sets and electric lights, but also industry as eventually factories and offices could be far more widely dispersed than in the days when they had to cluster round a single power source. The same was true of the internal combustion engine and the car. Again it took a good fifty to sixty years for cars to become a widespread possession in the major societies of the west, and only then did it become apparent just how much they were reshaping cities with the spread of suburbs and supermarkets, and the steady disappearance of the street and the old community based on walking. Indeed it is arguably only now in the 1990s that Britain is beginning to take on some of the character of the car-based cities of the USA, with edge cities, vast shopping malls and friendship patterns in which most neighbours are strangers.

The same slow pattern is happening with information technologies. My guess is that we are only half-way through the steady transformation of our own lives through them. Some of the barriers are still technological. We still can't easily control machines with our voices, although the last few years have at last brought rapid progress and it may not be long before the keyboard becomes a thing of the past. Machines still find it hard to talk to each other; the fantasy of being able to phone your home from the office and tell it to set the central heating, make a meal or send a message to your spouse is still a long way from becoming fact. Computers are still far from being able to learn very much, or to think, despite some dramatic advances in neural networking that mimics the human brain.

But the really important barriers in the way of IT achieving its full potential are social ones, just as they were with previous generations of technology. Few societies feel at ease with freely flowing information, for the simple reason that it means that not only can information flow about the capital of Outer Mongolia but also hard-core pornography, malicious gossip and personal health records. Within organisations, the most efficient use of information often depends on allowing it to flow far more freely than is the norm in most of them where scarce information is almost what defines people's power and authority. It has also proved far harder to dismantle the barriers between home and work than most IT enthusiasts expected – partly because employers still like direct control, and the shared culture of the office or factory, partly because employees depend so much on work for meeting other people.

When the social innovations start occurring, we shall find that this second phase of any technology's life can be far more disorienting than the first. At first, technologies can be fitted into familiar boxes. Cars were initially seen as horseless carriages. Electricity replaced gaslights. And the first computers replaced clerks doing repetitive jobs adding up the accounts or making it easier to type out a document – this was why their inventors believed that the world could get by with only four or five computers, and at most perhaps one for each country.

But the full rollout of generic technologies involves the radical creation and destruction of ways of doing things: not only jobs, but also organisations, types of culture, forms of power. Some of these are just coming into view. We are beginning to understand just how much technologies now make us visible – not only to closed circuit television cameras in shopping centres, but also to computers tracking where we shop, what we buy, whom we phone and what health treatments we have. We can already buy for a few hundred pounds on the black market other people's credit and shopping details, or transcripts of their telephone calls, and we will soon be able to buy ultra cheap surveillance equipment to spy on our girlfriends or boyfriends or protect our homes. We are beginning to learn that privacy gains quite a new meaning in an information-rich society, and that privacy law may need to be turned on its head in order to require firms and other big agencies to prove that they don't store any information on us without our approval.

These radical changes will undoubtedly be met with anguished horror by many. None of the changes will avoid heavy costs. And yet it is worth noticing that none of the earlier warnings (and promises) has truly been realised. Computers have brought in neither a push-button democracy nor a big brother superstate. Despite the warnings of mass unemployment that have been common since the 1960s, a higher, not lower, proportion of population is now in work. Despite the warnings of cultural destruction, which have also been with us for at least 30 years, more people read more books than ever before (partly because computers have cut costs in the publishing process).

It seems, however, that we have a particular need, in a pre-millennial decade, for simpler verities of hope or dread, of eager optimism and equally eager pessimism. Perhaps in an age of anxieties about everything from contaminated food to nerve-gas attacks, it is almost comforting to have the villain clearly visible and sitting on your desk.

Linda Grant

Violent Anxiety

*

When the war broke out in the former Yugoslavia, we in Britain were startled to find that otherwise sophisticated Europeans who owned VCRs and drank Diet Coke could go at each other with the same brutal gusto as our barbaric ancestors did in the Middle Ages. Then we put down the paper and went out to the pictures to watch *Terminator II*. Half the population of the world is running away from violence into refugee camps and the other half is paying good money to watch it at the multiplex. We have managed to separate the real from the imaginary into such watertight compartments that we can laugh at heads being blown off at the cinema while requiring trauma counselling if we arrive home to find we have been burgled.

We began the twentieth century with high hopes. A conjunction of developing technology and political liberalism held out the expectation that a continent which had always teetered on the brink of starvation could finally eliminate famine and disease and begin to engineer a happy life on earth rather than in heaven. Now we find ourselves approaching the end of what must have been the bloodiest of centuries: of mass death made possible by instruments of mass destruction; of the application of industrial methods of mass production to attempt to eliminate an entire ethnic minority; of a single bomb with the potential to wipe out the entire population of a nation. There is apparently no end to our capacity for barbarism. New technology only created new weapons.

Violence shows no signs of being on its way out of fashion, in England or abroad. The inflicting of pain on others (and more fashionably now, on oneself) has been in full spate in the nineties: in Bosnia, Rwanda and Northern Ireland, out on the streets at inner city riots, and more privately inside houses and cellars in county towns like Gloucester. With every new war it returns to startle us with the ferocity of its power and what seems to be our innate capacity to indulge it. There is no sign of its withering away either in the real world or in our hunger to see it depicted on the screen. We are, it seems, surrounded by violence; fear of it eats away at us. We are terrified of pain and suffering and we are fascinated by it.

To some extent violence, and our failed attempts to eradicate it, defines the twentieth century. Our notions of progress have in part been about the conviction that if only we could educate the masses out of superstition and savagery and bigotry we would automatically eliminate violence, and as we reach the close of the century we might want to ponder on why we have so spectacularly failed.

It is a very long time, fifty years, since Britain sent young men in any great numbers to die in a war, fifty years since any British town or city was raided from the skies. The IRA's bombing campaigns are too sporadic, random and thinly scattered across the mainland to impose on-going disruption to our daily routine. We have known a very long peace at home while being in the unique position to watch a continuous television documentary of wars and civil wars abroad – Vietnam, Biafra, Afghanistan, the Falklands, Iran–Iraq, the Gulf, Bosnia, Chechnya, to name only the chart-toppers, as it were, the ones we knew well enough to hum the words to, or rather be able to spell the names of the places in which they were happening and the leaders who perpetrated them. So why are we still so exercised about violence? Why do we ensure that we are not deprived of it in the form of TV and films, and why do we seek out painful and violent experiences? And is our widespread fear of crime in itself a kind of subconscious desire to continue to engage emotionally with pain?

I want to begin by suggesting that our individual responses to violence are very much informed by when we were born in the century, that there now exist three quite separate generations, each bringing to violence a different set of impulses: those who lived through it, don't talk about it and are only now beginning to engage publicly (and perhaps even privately) with the trauma of half a century ago; those who have never known it and want to engineer it socially out of existence; and those who have never known it but flirt with it as a new way to *épater les baby-boomers* as the boomers themselves once, in a memorable phrase, 'forced sex down everyone's throats'.

I fall into the middle category. For example: I was sitting in the dentist's waiting room, attending on what I expected (and proved to be) painful treatment for that scourge of middle age, receding gums, when I fell into conversation with another candidate for the chair, a youngish man who had recently started a new cinema. I asked him how it was going, and he said, pretty well. They were currently showing Quentin Tarantino's *Pulp Fiction* which was packing them in.

'Is it good?' I asked.

'It's brilliant,' he replied. 'There's a scene' – he began to laugh – 'God, it's so funny. There's these two gangsters and they've got this guy in the back of the car and there's a gun pointing at his head and they drive over a bump and *the gun goes off.* It blows his face away.' By now he was choking with laughter, wiping tears away.

I sat there with my mouth open. 'I don't get it,' I said. 'That's horrible. How is it funny?'

It took me some weeks to get to see *Pulp Fiction*. By that time I had heard perhaps half a dozen times about the hysterical scene when this guy in the back of a car gets his head blown off. I saw it on a wet night between Christmas and New Year. I sat tensely, waiting for laughter to be forced out of me against my will. I didn't laugh once, not even in the scene when the man gets his head blown off. Not only did I not laugh, I shut my eyes because I thought it was so horrible. What is the matter with you? my friends asked contemptuously. For heaven's sake, it's only a *film*. Have you not pondered Quentin Tarantino's words when accused of having too much blood in his films? – 'That's not blood, it's red.' (Actually it was Jean-Paul Godard who said that first.)

For them, violence is spectacle. Their discerning eyes critically assess the professionalism of the maquillage which creates the illusion that someone has had their head blown off. What might make me scream and close my eyes makes some other viewers disdainfully dismiss second-rate special effects. Try as I might, it always looks like blood to me, not ketchup. My disbelief is always willingly suspended. Theirs has to be coaxed. 'All is illusion,' they cry. 'But see if you can persuade me otherwise.'

My response would be explicable if I had no sense of humour, but violence has become slightly less funny to me after reading that teenage audiences in Los Angeles giggled their way through *Schindler's List*, not because they were neo-Nazis but because they could no longer recognise what was supposed to be serious and what was not, and who can blame them? Violent action films are designed not to send us screaming home to bed, but to entertain us. Yet I had to ask myself, after *Pulp Fiction*, can one be visually literate, wise to irony and the notion that there is no reality, only different forms of representation, and *still* hate violence? Can one exist at all in the modern world like this? I hate violence, and do not approve of it in exactly the same manner that the previous generation did not like and did not approve of sex. Like London taxi-drivers on the subject of more or less everything, I think there should be a law against it. And like those who ring the BBC to complain about 'bad language', perhaps I am an irrelevant and embarrassingly outdated throw-back.

This aversion does not apply to sex, of course: you could show gay fist-fucking live on tea-time television and I wouldn't be all that bothered but I don't like boxing, I don't like horror films or action films or war films, I don't like sado-masochism and I don't like guns or knives or piercing instruments. I don't mind news photographs or television footage of the aftermath of violence – the mutilated and bleeding bodies, the gouged-out eyes – because I believe that this kind of thing ought to put people off violence and I don't like to think that they might actually get off on it.

As part of the first generation of the twentieth century not to have been alive during a world war, I have had almost no direct experience of violence myself, yet this very generation has extended the definition of it to cover activities which were not formerly defined as violent acts: boxing and hunting which used to be sports are now violence;

eating meat which used to be good nutrition is now violence; wearing fur which was a sign of wealth is now violence; rape which used to be bad sex is now nothing to do with sex and everything about violence; being hit by one's husband used to be part of bad marriages to no-good men, now it is domestic violence; bottom-pinching which used to be flirtation is now violence; angry words which were once part of argument are now verbal violence. My violence-free generation sees violence everywhere we look as the Victorians, espying table legs, found them immodest and somehow euphemistic.

If I were sixty and talking the way I do about *sex*, a younger me would accuse myself of having a problem, that I was actually sexually repressed, and maybe that is true. Perhaps my squeamishness conceals a submerged fascination with violence and pain, which, were I only to unlock and explore it, would make me happier and healthier, less hung-up. This has been the argument behind the transformation of sado-masochism from a secretive sexual sub-cult to a practice that has surfaced as a gay response to the requirements of safe sex and has now insinuated its way into mainstream fashion, as rubber dresses and bondage wear began to appear on the catwalks ending up in the high street. The fashion for piercing and tattooing began in S/M clubs like London's Torture Garden and wound up in the suburbs with piercing studios commonplace in county towns. Sado-masochism is now a routine part of mainstream pornography rather than a sub-genre. Madonna's stage act has been full of it for years. One of the photographs in *Vanity Fair*'s TV Hall of Fame depicted Mary Tyler Moore as a dominatrix 'riding' Dick van Dyke, who was down on all fours. The photograph was titled 'The Nineties Couple', a knowing reference to the squeaky-clean husband and wife of the fifties and sixties which they used to portray. It was sad to see them got up like that.

Oddly, while definitions of violence are busy colonising large areas of activity, we are also being asked to withdraw that definition from other places such as consensual sado-masochistic sex. What used to be grievous bodily harm, such as genital 'torture' with nails and scalpels, is now sex. Putting a bolt through one's scrotum, which used to be self-mutilation, is now sex. Requiring someone to be shackled, which used to be slavery, is now sex.

My own primal '*No!*' when faced with the piercer's needle, I was told by one piercer, was a symptom of the modern world's attempt to run away from pain, to anaesthetise ourselves against it instead of seeking out the intense experience, the one in which you know, completely, that you are alive and not dead. So pain, it seems, has taken over from or perhaps accompanies drugs – my generation's sensitiser – as a new means of acquiring heightened consciousness and sensation.

It is no wonder that three generations squirm uncomfortably when confronted with the definitions of the other. We still know shockingly little about the effects the Second World War had on those who fought and lived through it. Veterans' organisations at the time of the VE Day commemorations talked of how the anniversary had triggered off memories of unresolved traumas in many of their members, that they had more work to do rather than less. Few people now in their seventies could have made it through from 1939 to 1945 without someone close to them being killed.

My own response to violence, like that of many of my generation, seems to have been formed out of separate but intermeshing influences: first, being brought up by people who had spent their teens and twenties in air-raid shelters or trying to kill someone else before he killed you. Post-war children, we saw around us the evidence of the bombing in the shattered houses and gaps along the street, and were terrified that it might start up again. What might have provided adventure and opportunity for our parents, just sounded scary to many of us. And if, like me, you were Jewish, you could not credit that you had been born after that nightmare had ended (though well aware that had it continued much longer, one would not have been born at all and that one's parents would have long ago gone up in smoke.) Yet we lacked any actual experience of violence which might put it into some kind of perspective, to normalise it or charge it with significance as returning servicemen could, with pride, boast that they had helped to defeat fascism. Nor for me was real death all that near; not one member of my family died until I was in my teens.

A second factor shaping my inhibitions about violence was the development of a feminist response to what was defined as 'male violence' – from the male-dominated military industrial complex to the male-dominated pharmaceutical complex. We were the ones who, in the seventies, defined rape and sexual abuse and sexual harassment as violence, established women's refuges and rape counselling centres, lobbied for better street-lighting or set up women-driver cab companies. We were the ones who rebelled against industrial methods of childbirth and chose drug-free deliveries and were *amazed* to discover that it actually hurt a great deal. But as pain went it was 'natural', which was good, so we put up with it. We did not define it as violence; perhaps as piercing is a means of flirting with pain, natural childbirth may also be a means to seek out profound sensation. We were the generation who ludicrously suggested that 'Mother Nature' was warm, caring and beneficent and peaceful. Tell that to the victim of an earthquake.

Finally, my generation's response to violence is informed by our fear of crime. In an essay of this nature this might be the moment to imply that our preoccupation with crime is somehow a form of moral panic, that there is no basis for our anxiety, that this is another example of the middle classes getting worked up about something that masks real fears about something else. But before we assume that, I want to ask first whether it is true that there is more violence in society than there used to be, or if it is just that everyone *feels* this to be the case. Sections of the media feed the idea that there once was a golden age which was crime free, when you could go down to your local and leave the back door open and when you got home everything was just as you left it. It is probably true that there was far less burglary and car theft during the thirties and forties because there was far less to nick, particularly from the homes of the poor, whereas nowadays a thief can more or less rely on there being a colour television anywhere he (or, extremely rarely, she) breaks into.

But we are not the first generation to be fearful of walking the streets. A very early moral panic about violence occurred in the 1860s when there was a outbreak of garotting. The population of the metropolis lived in so much terror that advertisements began to appear for special anti-garotting collars. 'Garotting is the talk of the town, penal jurisprudence the favourite after-dinner topic', a journalist wrote in the *Illustrated London News* for 29 November 1862.[1] Were the men and women of the 1860s right to believe that there was more violent crime about then than in the past? Actually, yes. The highest ever recorded figure for homicide occurred in 1865 – 414 or 19.6 per million of the British population, compared with the all-time low in 1918, when murders accounted for only 6.1 per million,[2] perhaps because those with a penchant for killing had signed up early for the mass carnage and were already dead. Homicide rates were low between the wars and during the fifties, and did not begin to rise until the seventies, doing so slowly, rather than alarmingly, reaching 14.1 per thousand of the population in 1994, the last year for which the Home Office has figures. So yes, there is more violent crime now than there has been in living memory, though whether we are right to panic is another matter.

What was the actual number of murders in 1994? It was 729. That is how many people were murdered in England and Wales. It isn't a lot. What is the likelihood of a reader of this sentence having known anyone who has been murdered? How many people do you know who know someone who has murdered? On the whole, murder barely touches our lives, like the jackpot on the National Lottery. The two are similar in their randomness: it *could* be you. But it's very, very unlikely.

So why are we so worried, and who is doing the worrying? We can correctly deduce that we worry more about crime because we are more aware of it. The part of London in which I live has a local paper which displays a hoarding outside all the local newsagents. Virtually every single week the headline is a crime story – a rape, a mugging, an armed robbery or a murder – even when that story may be found in the actual paper buried away in one paragraph at the bottom of page two. A friend who has lived in the area longer than I have pointed out that, ten years ago, week after week the hoarding displayed 'loony left' local government stories. Perhaps the council became more responsible, perhaps the loony left story went out of fashion. Unerringly, the editors knew that beneath this brief interest in how our ratepayer's money was being spent was a reserve of preoccupation with crime that could always be tapped when nothing else very interesting was going on. So are the media to blame for exacerbating our fear of crime? If so, newspaper bosses have a great deal of previous. In 1866 50 per cent of the content of a London newspaper called *Lloyd's Weekly News* dealt with crime. Crime stories are those which carry a high 'through reading score', that is, readers carry on to the end rather than skimming the first paragraph. So editors are not exactly force-feeding us material we would rather turn away from.[3]

I want to suggest that violence forms our greatest anxiety now because the crimes we currently fear strike at the heart of our private lives. Unlike the anxiety of the Victorians, which was directed to street crime, we fear what might happen in the sanctuary of our own homes. A number of murders in the past quarter of a century have had a particular and peculiar effect on the public psyche. They fall into three categories: the murder of women, the murder of children and murders by children. I do not believe that the population is unduly exercised by fatalities outside pubs in which both parties are drunk, or by gangland shootings between different Yardie factions. There have always been gangsters at the movies; we know all about them. They are organised. Let them shoot each other to death if they like, as in the last scene of *Reservoir Dogs* (a Tarantino film I did laugh at) in which a circle of hoodlums each has a gun pointed at another's head. They all fire simultaneously and that's the end of them. Rather quarrelsome gangsters than lone woman-hating psychotics of whom the neighbours ritually say, 'he kept himself to himself'.

When I consider the violent crime that terrorised my own childhood in the fifties, three cases stand out: the Christie and Evans case (an early House of Horrors), Ruth Ellis, James Hanratty and the Derek Bentley case (Bentley and Evans would later receive public pardons). It has been suggested that two of them, Ellis and Bentley, fascinated the public at the time because they appeared in the guise of glamorous outlaws, one a night-club hostess, the other an early version of a teddy boy in suede shoes and gangster drapes. In other words, they spoke to the public's fears of the challenge by a youth sub-culture to authority in the case of Bentley, and the challenge to a woman's position as wife and housewife, in the case of Ellis.

The crimes that have haunted us since the sixties are: the Moors Murders, the Mary Bell case, the Yorkshire Ripper, Dennis Nilsen, the abduction of the estate agent Suzy Lamplugh, the murder of Rachel Nickell, the Bulger case, the child murders by Robert Black and the West case. It is too soon to say whether the Dunblane massacre of school children will join this list. Already Hungerford has faded from memory. It seems that lone gun-men, who carry out a single assault, however savage, on a general population, come into the category of events to which we cannot assign a great deal of meaning. Thomas Hamilton seems to have killed because he was consistently denied paedophilic access to young boys; his guns were licensed. He was law-abiding. What, people ask helplessly, could have been done to prevent this crime? Probably nothing.

The gangland murders committed by the Krays and the near-murder in the Great Train Robbery are now nostalgic memories of a time when our very own criminals behaved like Yanks. Neither the Krays nor the Great Train Robbers were lone misfits but professionals, woven in to the fabric of their communities, even exercising a form of order and structure on them. We may disapprove of the murder of policemen and other officials, but by and large we believe that being subject to such danger is part of the job. We are no longer outraged by challenges to authority, to the public realm; now our fear is directed at violence invading our own private territory. which accounts for the impact of films such as *Cape Fear* and *Fatal Attraction* in which the family is depicted as a fortress under assault.

The effect of the child murders, whether committed by adults or children themselves, has had a simple effect: that of severely restricting children's freedom so that many reach their early teens having never negotiated public transport. The murders of women pose a greater problem. All the women who died, whether the university student Lucy Partington who, it is believed, accepted a lift from the Wests because she had missed the last bus, or Suzy Lamplugh going about her business as an estate agent, were out in the world without male protection. They died, perhaps, because they were not fast at home inside the kitchen, with children and neighbours close by and a husband there at night. The Ripper's first victims were prostitutes; a number of the bodies found in Gloucester Road were never really missed or reported as missing: girls who had been in care or just took off one day after a job and were just assumed to be not around any more.

Part of my own fear of violence is a terror that, like Rachel Nickell, I might be walking in a park in broad daylight and be beaten to death or that I will be at home asleep and someone will break down my expensive anti-burglar defences and kill me and *no man will be there to protect me*. I think of the young, single woman doctor living in a basement flat in St John's Wood who was killed on Boxing Day 1994 by an intruder who has never been caught. Women feel more vulnerable because we are more free and, unprotected, prone to violence. At the end of 1995 the French au pair, Céline Figard, was murdered, having been last seen taking a lift from a lorry driver in the south of England. The police attempted to see if Figard's death could be linked to those of a number of other women whose bodies had been found, naked, at the sides of roads. The press began to ask if there was another serial killer about. But the *Guardian*'s Duncan Campbell asked a far more frightening question: instead of a single serial killer, might it not be more disturbing if there was no link at all? '. . . that there are many, many men carrying out these murders. And that means we could be drifting into the kind of world where little self-appointed one-man death squads consisting of our most embittered and violent misogynists . . . now feel free to murder almost casually.'[4]

Perhaps, then, it is women, both as potential victims and as mothers of potential victims, who have been partly responsible for generating the fear of violence. Going about more in the world we have discovered that the world is a more woman-hating and dangerous place than we had thought. Maybe it's significant that, unlike men, we lack a culture to contain and even enjoy it. On the whole, women don't go to boxing matches or other spectacles of violence to work off our aggression because we don't have that much aggression to begin with. Though women are watching action and horror movies in increasingly large numbers, our obsession with violence does not go into its simulation but into worrying about it. The number of women involved in an offence involving violence against the person has doubled in the past decade to 9400 a year, and the average daily prison population of females jailed for violent crimes has jumped from 240 in 1992 to 360 in 1995, though these are still tiny figures compared to male offenders. Even when women are using crack or mug someone with a weapon they tend to do so as accomplices to men, usually boyfriends or husbands. Very few women have murdered for pecuniary motives and rarely, if ever, without a male presence. Of *course* we are shocked by a Rosemary West or a Myra Hindley, for their crimes do indeed seem to fly in the face of nature.

We have long seen violence as coming from three directions – from war, from organised crime and from the unmanageable margins of society, such as the escaped mental patient or the lone gunman. The murder of the headteacher Philip Lawrence by a gang of teenagers young enough to still be in school tells us that violence now pervades everyday life. But we should have known that already. In the eighties we discovered the extent of child abuse and, in doing so, we had our noses ground in a rank-smelling mess. Violence does not always assault the family from outside but is inherent in it; for many, the family is the hell from which they have to escape.

The two most spectacular crimes of the nineties were the murder of the toddler Jamie Bulger and the serial killings carried out by Fred and Rosemary West. During each trial the newspapers chose to focus on what the murders meant in terms of the breakdown of community and the collapse of the family. But these were false signals. Over thirty people saw or stopped Jon Venables and Robert Thompson as they made their way through Walton to the railway line and a grotesque although passionless killing, which, it was suggested, was copied from a horror video they had seen at home. Countless times they were asked what they were doing out alone and where they were taking the little boy in their company. When they said he was lost and they were taking him to the police station, one woman even offered to accompany them.

Similarly, neither Fred nor Rosemary West came from 'broken homes', neither did they divorce. They were, on the surface, a happily married couple with a large brood of children. For Anne-Marie West who survived her childhood, but hardly intact, the family was not a place of refuge from a violent world but the source of violence. In other ways the Wests appear a modern couple with an open marriage and, according to accounts of the case, they regarded themselves as having 'healthy', unrepressed attitudes to sex. Yet at the heart of the marriage was a preoccupation with violence, with sado-masochism which they took to its logical conclusion. What seems very chic when frothed into a confection by Jean-Paul Gaultier was a nightmare for the Wests' victims. Fred and Rosemary should never have been let near S/M; it is for those who need violence as representation, who have never known it. In the childhoods of both the Wests, violence was never far off.

The media chose not to report fully what went on at the trials of Venables and Thompson and Rosemary West. In the first case, this was partly because some evidence never came to court on the grounds that it might unduly upset the Bulger family; during the West trial a number of newspaper editors believed that the public could not handle the truth. They chose to censor their accounts not from fear of copycat crimes but because what actually happened was unbearable. Everyone involved in the trial was offered counselling, including the journalists.

The even more ghastly truth about these two cases, the most unpalatable of all, is not that they are symptoms of social breakdown but that they occurred where both community and family was still intact. It wasn't an 'uncle' who murdered Heather West, it was her own mother and father. The Bulger killers weren't lone misfits; each had a mum and a dad and went to school, and the families were locally known. They didn't sneak out to watch horror videos – one of their dads rented them for them. Violence *is* all around us, in familiar places. It isn't spawned by social breakdown: it was there all along.

Earlier I said that it was usual to dismiss any form of anxiety as a moral panic, that it almost always masks a fear of something else. Anxiety about violence may be really a fear about social dissolution; or it might anticipate the great act of violence that is to come – our own deaths. For we are all to be killed one day, whether on the street or at work or in our bed or, more likely, in hospital with blood and pain and well-intentioned nurses and doctors and our family standing by helpless to prevent it. There is a current theory that we have reached the end of the Enlightenment, the belief in progress, cleanliness and order. From the eighteenth century onwards we swore to combat disease, decay, superstition. We have replaced the maggot-filled coffin with the electric crematorium so that the grave cannot gape and the dead rise. We have transformed the pierced body of Christ into gentle Jesus meek and mild. Yet it is our own twentieth century that took the technology of the cinema, applied it to the medieval fascination with the dead, and used it to create the genre of the horror film. Have the last hundred years of war served to inform us that the Enlightenment, instead of sweeping away illusions, was the biggest chimera of all? Has this last decade with its body-piercing and sado-masochism been a reminder that an engagement with violence is so built in to the psyche that we have to find some form or other to express it: by actually committing a violent act; taking part in it vicariously; or by worrying about it?

Perhaps my own problem with films like *Pulp Fiction* and *Cape Fear* is that given a childhood with a far too early immersion in the history of the holocaust, I simply internalised the horror into my own dark places and I don't need to go to the movies. Of the concentration camps, George Steiner wrote: 'There were regulated gradations of horror within the total concentric sphere. *L'univers concentrationnaire* has no true counterpart in the secular mode. Its analogue is Hell.'[5] When we attempt to imagine the deliberate – what Steiner calls the 'gratuitous' – terror inflicted on camp inmates and now the victims of the Wests in the place of endless night below the stairs, we see that the cellar, with its instruments of torture, like Belsen, was hell. 'They are,' Steiner wrote, 'the transference of Hell from below the earth to its surface.'

Yet we don't have Hell any more; we have abolished it along with religion so that we could replace Heaven with a secular utopia. Steiner wrote:[6]

> Much has been said of man's bewilderment and solitude after the disappearance of Heaven from active belief. We know of the natural emptiness of the skies and of the terrors it has brought. But it may be that the loss of Hell is the more severe dislocation. It may be that the mutation of Hell into metaphor left a formidable gap in the co-ordinates of location, of psychological recognition in the western world . . . To have neither Heaven nor Hell is to be intolerably deprived in a world gone flat. Of the two, Hell proved the easier to re-create. The pictures had always been more detailed.

Perhaps that is the explanation for our ambivalent relationship with violence. Maybe we need Hell. Men in uniform polishing their guns, women giving birth in chosen agony, couples sticking sharp objects into one another, writers compulsively re-telling the story of the Holocaust – we can only live in a world that is not free of pain and violence and death which, our instincts tell us, is only natural. In worrying about violence, we are at least true to ourselves. Violence is and always has been the state we are in. Whether it is the lawless mob, the skinhead, the football hooligan, the Yardie or whatever deviants currently present themselves to embody our fears, it is actually ourselves we are frightened of. We are frightened of what we are capable of. In Bosnia, neighbours of forty years turned their guns on each other. If Germany had invaded Britain in 1941, which stout English yeoman would have manned the ovens?

If we believe that violence inhabits the territory of anti-logic then to defeat violence by investigating it, by explaining it out of existence, is a paradox, an impossibility. To conquer violence may be to overthrow the self in the process. But as Steiner so presciently put it more than a quarter of a century ago:[7]

> We cannot turn back. We cannot choose the dreams of unknowing. We shall, I expect, open the last door in the castle even if it leads, perhaps *because* it leads, on to realities which are beyond the reach of human comprehension . . . To be able to envisage possibilities of self-destruction yet press home the debate with the unknown, is no mean thing.

Notes

1 This and subsequent references to garotting outbreaks are taken from Rob Sindall, *Street Violence in the Nineteenth Century*, University of Leicester Press, 1990, p.50.

2 These and subsequent crime figures provided by the Home Office, January 1996.

3 Sindall, op. cit., pp.33-4.

4 Duncan Campbell, 'Most Foul', *Guardian*, 3 January 1996.

5 George Steiner, *In Bluebeard's Castle: Some Notes Towards the Re-Definition of Culture*, Faber, 1971, p.47.

6 Ibid., p.48.

7 Ibid., p.106.

Mary Midgley

Earth Matters: Thinking about the Environment

How Environmental Alarm Arose

What did we worry about before we started to worry about the environment? And did we worry in a different style?

Looking back as this book's most ancient contributor, I don't think that there has ever been, in my time, any shortage of worry, any lack of grit to form pearls in the mental oyster. To my generation, born in Europe shortly after the First World War, the central alarm was fear either of the Nazis or of the Bolsheviks according to taste. For myself, with an eye on the Nazis, this fear was certainly overshadowing, and I don't now think that it was unreasonable. It merged, of course, into the fear of another disastrous war, a war of conquest which one or both of these ideologies might launch against the rest of the world.

In short, we were still occupied by the fear of human hostility and destructiveness. This has, of course, been one of the two main fears that have kept people awake throughout human history, the other being the fear of natural disaster. I think that most of us moved only gradually from this human-centred fear to a wider alarm about the natural world. Many made this journey, as I did myself, by way of a concern about the nuclear menace. We noticed, first, that atomic explosions caused much longer-lasting damage than other kinds of weapon did, and only later – with a start of surprise – that there were other recent and widely-used inventions, such as pesticides, whose ill-effects were equally lasting. From there we went on to notice the exhaustion of resources and gradually understood the scale of the problem. Rachel Carson's books *Silent Spring* and *The Sea Around Us* were a landmark here.

Were we extraordinarily slow in grasping these obvious facts? I think that perhaps we were. Clear-sighted prophets had after all predicted this kind of trouble much earlier. Some indeed did so from the early days of the industrial revolution. Mary Shelley wrote a story called 'The Last Man', about the possibility of human extinction, and, as science-fiction developed, other fantasies on that theme appeared from time to time.

The Difficulty of Expecting the End of the World

So perhaps we were slow in the uptake. Yet the psychological change required to take this kind of thinking seriously was indeed a large and strange one, both in scale and in kind. Traditional alarms, both about human enemies and natural disasters, were usually fairly local. Mostly, people feared specific attack by their own enemies or specific damage to their own settlements and harvests. Or at most, they feared for a particular empire. This does not mean, of course, that the people themselves were necessarily less disturbed. For themselves and those around them, these threats were lethal. You can drown just as well in seven feet of water as you can in seventy. But people did not usually expect the end of the whole world, nor even a disaster to it such as a mass extinction. This does make a difference to the kind of alarm that we feel.

It is true that there were also panics from time to time about the end of the world, but these panics were somewhat exceptional and provoked an exceptional kind of thinking. They arose specially at times of general disturbance, such as the Napoleonic wars, or in response to particular ominous events, such as comets or the end of the First Millennium. When these crises did arise, the Christian tradition located them firmly in the context of the prophetic books of the Bible, especially *Revelations* and *Daniel*. Against this background the end of the physical world figured as something which, though terrible, must be passively accepted. It was an outcome that could not possibly be affected by human action. Human responses to it might be agonising but they were wholly an internal, spiritual concern.

By contrast, today even the most optimistic of us sees reason to expect damage which is not local – which will extend far beyond our own settlements – and which yet seems not to be an Act of God but avoidable human damage. It looks in principle as if we should be able to do something about it. Our settlements themselves, too, extend and interconnect in a way that was previously unknown, so that disasters cannot easily be seen as limited. We seem required to think (as people say) *globally*, just as much as earlier people were when they thought about the end of the world. But we are also expected – as they were not – to think practically, to reflect in a way that can somehow lead to preventive action. And it is really hard to combine these two perspectives.

The Pull of Fantasy

I am not here to discuss the various practical aspects of this crisis in the outside world, nor the particular actions that we might take about them. Other contributors to this volume are doing that. Instead I am gravitating (as is my habit) to the psychological side of the issue, because if we neglect that, we often cannot deal with the other aspects either. I want to discuss the special kind of anxiety that this situation provokes and the difficulty of envisaging this whole situation at all.

The trouble here is that efforts to think globally tend to get unrealistic. They merge easily into fantasy. We can see how readily this happens when we notice how some American fundamentalists are now reacting to current crises by taking off into the colourful visions provided by those very prophetic books of the Bible. The extent to which they claim to take these visions seriously seems to exceed that of most people in earlier ages. They invoke the imminent end of the world, not just as part of a call to repentance but as a practical consideration affecting policy. They treat it as an excuse for not taking action to deal with environmental damage. Current destruction is (they say) just part of the disasters which are due to accompany the end of the world. This destruction cannot be prevented and – since that end is indeed at hand – it does not really matter anyway.

This excuse may, of course, often be made in bad faith. It may owe a good deal to the rival ambition of various competing politicians and tele-evangelists. Nevertheless, I think that the strong appeal of this fatalism for ordinary people is still remarkable. Evidently, these people are more repelled by the difficulty of treating large-scale damage realistically as something that must be dealt with than they are by the many repulsive features of their own vision of the world as about to end.

We can surely understand this reaction. The more practical, realistic alternative does indeed look dauntingly strange. This move of supposing disaster possible upsets a background assumption about progress on which we have all grown up – an assumption which goes much deeper than our recent attempts to debunk it. It suggests that (as it were) the bus of technology, which we supposed was carrying us safely forward for ever, has stopped. We are being asked to notice that this bus is no longer going the right way and indeed that it has already gone some distance on the wrong one.

Anyone who has had to get off a bus in these circumstances will recognise how upsetting the change can be. It is not just that practical difficulties will follow. What bites most is the social effect. We are deprived of a reassuring ambience that has been taking all the decisions for us. We no longer have a driver who knows the way nor a set of fellow-passengers who can assure us that he is right. So if, at this point, another bus turns up which has not only a suitably confident driver but also a projector showing a colourful and reassuring film about the route that this bus will follow, we shall naturally be inclined to climb aboard. This seems to be what has happened to the American fundamentalists. But if you will forgive me, I should like to follow this bus metaphor a little further because I think it has something to say about other predicaments besides theirs.

In the first place, it involves an important and influential group of people who would certainly never travel by bus – members of governments, captains of industry and others who consider themselves to be currently running the world. Though these people are in general well-educated, they have been very slow to take environmental considerations on board as a ground for policy. No doubt most of them would not suppose that they have much in common with the naive fundamentalists that I just mentioned. All the same, inside their first-class railway carriage – or their chauffeur-driven Rolls – a cinema-projector is also running.

The film that this projector shows is just as unlike current reality as the apocalyptic one. In its commonest form, this film is a soothing affair which simply shows a loop repeating the past. In its more enterprising and ideological form, it shows these repetitions as changing gradually under the benign influence of market forces into a new kind of civilisation which will transport current states and those who rule them, without essential change, to even grander heights. The guiding theme in both visions is economism – the belief that a particular exchange system finally determines everything. Capitalism – exactly like Marxism – is held to tap, by its monetary system, an unfailing source of energy which is sure to see us right in the end.

Visions Are Not a Luxury

Part of my point here is obvious enough. It is simply that what makes it hard for powerful people to grasp environmental dangers is not just the practical fact that their lives are largely insulated from painful effects of these dangers. More deeply, it is the social and psychological fact that they share a *dream* with a group of influential people whom they take to be authoritative on all important questions. Their tribal commitment to this group is sealed by a shared imaginative vision. That vision is self-perpetuating because anyone who questions it automatically becomes suspect and is eventually excluded from the authorative group. Eminent politicians like Robert McNamara or

Nobel-prize-winning scientists like the late Linus Pauling who begin to denounce the common creed are quickly seen as eccentrics and disregarded.

From the outside, we, who do not travel on those privileged forms of transport, can often see this selective process very clearly. What, however, do we, who *do* worry about the environment, want to say about our own position? We know that we too are accused of ignoring reality, of being driven by dreams and visions. We need to think what this accusation amounts to.

It is important to grasp that visions as such are not a mere distraction from practical life but an organic part of it. They are a set of signposts that decide its direction. The reason why 'without vision the people perish' is simply that without it they cannot move at all. They are paralysed. The moral of my metaphor (then) is not that we should never use a bus, since we may well often need to travel together. Nor is it that we should never show a film on our bus, never entertain a colourful vision which shows the point of our journey. The moral is just that we need to be aware of what these things are doing for us psychologically. There is a crucial difference between – on the one hand – ideals which are consciously entertained, expressed in an appropriate vision, able to change under criticism, and – on the other – obsessive, uncriticised fantasies. It goes with the difference between deliberate, thoughtful support for a chosen group and blind, tribal, habit-driven adherence to a particular party.

We all need visions. We all have them. The point is not that we should kill our imaginations so as to deal only in facts. It is that we need to be aware of the visions so as to choose the ways in which they develop. In alarming and disturbing times, various things easily go wrong with this process. The most obvious of them is escapism. Both of the bad fantasies that I have mentioned are designed, in their very different ways, to minimise anxiety by imposing a numbing, sedative vision. One of these visions treats disaster as impossible, so that no effort is necessary. The other treats disaster as unavoidable, which makes all effort useless. Can we somehow find a workable position between these extremes? Can we somehow manage to accept some degree of worry and use it creatively?

Looking around us we can see that this can in fact be done. There are, and have always been, heroic people who insist on treating the evils of their time as curable by trying to cure them, and who thereby change people's perception in a way that actually makes some degree of cure possible. To give just one example, the early nineteenth-century reformers who attacked industrial slavery did so in the face not only of vested interests but also of a strong and impressive vision, expressed in theories of political economy, which claimed to show scientifically that their project was impossible. They had to fight this vision in two ways, both intellectually by arguing about the facts and imaginatively by providing a different vision.

These are both anxious enterprises and some of those reformers (notably Lord Shaftesbury) were very anxious people. They did, however, manage to use their anxiety creatively, taking advantage of its ferment to stir the imaginative pool in a way that brought new and constructive elements in it to the top. They produced (as it were) better and more realistic films to show on the communal bus.

On Not Wasting Anxiety

Our need at the end of the twentieth century is surely, first, to draw attention to this imaginative function of anxiety – to the possibility of using it constructively in changing the communal vision – and then to attend to the particular current visions which we now need to change if we are to make more room for awareness of the environment.

To start, then, with the more general point – Anxiety has a function. It is not just an illness nor is it (as Freud so oddly thought) a useless side-effect of sexual repression. As ethnologists have pointed out, it is a state of heightened arousal which fairly complex animals, especially the more intelligent ones, regularly display when they find themselves in frustrating situations. The arousal provides a reserve of energy. It keeps them on their toes looking for ways to circumvent the frustration. It is a natural response to conflict, both to conflict with the outer world and to inner conflict between one's own motives. In both cases, it is a much more useful response than a mere collapse into submission.

Certainly anxiety can become excessive, and when it finds no practical outlet it can also become destructive. The arousal then leads to activity which is wasteful and damaging, or it can be directed inwards to produce troubles such as gastric ulcers. But this only happens when intelligence has multiplied the visions without managing to find an activity that will employ this extra energy.

Intelligence itself is therefore a mixed blessing here. Its fertility can easily multiply difficulties in a way that is actually harmful. Not surprisingly, *Homo Sapiens Sapiens* is very susceptible to this misfortune. Any creature clever enough to perceive all its dangers is liable to get so interested in them that it becomes unable to find a way through them. This fertility in worry is indeed often a grave impediment to all kinds of change. Accordingly, some very effective reformers have been relatively thick-skinned, non-worrying people whose intelligence does not give them this kind of trouble. These people seem to operate rather as Perseus did when he managed to kill the Gorgon without actually looking at her. He used a highly-polished shield like a driving-mirror so that he only saw her reflection in isolation, and this reflection did not turn him to stone as the direct sight of her would have done.

This kind of narrow concentration on particular objectives is indeed one essential strategy when we are trying to make changes. We cannot afford to worry about everything. But it needs, of course, to be balanced by a wider vision which has surveyed the whole scene so as to choose the central point to be attacked. To drop the metaphors – in order to change the unreal, fantasy-ridden way in which people today are accustomed to view their world, we have to grasp the general shape of their vision clearly. We must not, ourselves, be led away by over-simple fantasies about some particular thing that is wrong in their thinking.

Avoiding Simple Wars

It is not very helpful (for instance) to rely, as some people do, on the simple idea that all our troubles are caused by religion, so that if once we got rid of that everything would go swimmingly. Nor indeed is it much use to entertain the alternative hope – as another set of people is beginning to do today – that we could similarly cure all our evils by getting rid of science. These simple notions both spring from an outdated tribal battle. Our ideas of both religion and science are at present absurdly stereotyped as a result of quarrels at the end of the nineteenth century. People like T.H.Huxley then contended against ecclesiastics to get science properly taught in schools. In reply, some evangelical Christians began seriously to defend Creationism as a factual doctrine. Each party saw the other as mindless, confirming a strange idea of 'science' and 'religion' as alternative complete world-views.

This is rather like having a map of Europe which shows Italy and Sweden as rival empires competing to dominate the whole. No doubt there have been times, such as the height of the Roman Empire or the reign of Gustavus Adolphus, when there could have been a point in thinking this way. But most of the time the other provinces of the intellectual world (which correspond to the rest of Europe) set the scene within which these two aspects of life find their role. Any complete vision of the world has to contain a place for both science and religion. They are complementary. Italy and Sweden may be far apart, but Europe needs both of them.

The idea that religious attitudes are optional is, I am sure, a mistake. It is a mistake that flows from defining religion far too narrowly – in fact, it commonly flows from equating it with official public worship and indeed with fundamentalist Christianity. By contrast, we can see how complementary these two aspects of life really are in the confusions that have surrounded James Lovelock's vision of the earth as Gaia. Lovelock suggested that we should think of the earth as Gaia – a name which the Greeks used for their earth-mother-goddess – as a way of bringing home to people the wholeness, the sacredness and the vulnerability of the planet. (The name was actually suggested to him by his neighbour, the novelist William Golding.)

This move at once struck the public imagination and has evidently succeeded in carrying just the message that he had intended. But it also shocked many atheistical scientists, and some Christians too, because they considered it superstitious. The trouble is that this benign and useful concept unmistakably has both a scientific and a religious side, and this is something we are quite unused to.

Lovelock himself – who is above all a solid atmospheric chemist - has been extremely cautious about the religious side of it. Indeed he has sometimes said that he wishes he had never made this suggestion, no doubt because of the stupid stereotyping just mentioned. But the inhibitions which block this recognition today are not rational.

To consider the world – and indeed the universe – which we inhabit with awe, reverence and respect is entirely reasonable. Most of the great scientists have expressed just this kind of reverent attitude to nature. And the particular twist which Lovelock has added to this reverence by his scientific work – by establishing the detailed continuity that exists between the living and the non-living parts of our planet – is indeed very well expressed by saying that we are *akin* to it, that it is our parent. By this image, he has radically undermined Descartes' picture of the human soul as standing above and apart from a contemptible kind of matter that was merely an object to it, wholly dead and inert.

This Cartesian picture is still very powerful in the minds of scientists. Yet it is radically at odds with today's scientific beliefs about our evolutionary origins. And it constantly blocks our attempts to take in how much the non-human environment matters. It produces a distorted world-view which we urgently need to change – the unbalanced, exclusive exaltation of the human race as something separate from the rest of nature.

The Dual Roles of Christianity and the Enlightenment

Historically, this absurd self-worship does not derive only from science or only from religion. It has roots both in the earlier, Christian phase of our culture and in the later, secular kind of thinking developed in the eighteenth century which goes under the name of the Enlightenment, a way of thinking we now see as centring on science. The new and better vision which we need to substitute for it will also need to draw on roots from both those traditions, because both are central to our culture. Wholesale warfare against either Christianity or the Enlightenment will get us nowhere. There is no possibility of jumping right off our historical roots and inventing a quite new world-view. We have to use what we have got and use it differently.

It is interesting to see how complex each of these roots is. Christian thinking has indeed worked in many ways to exclude the rest of nature from human concern. Even more strongly than Judaism, Christianity has concentrated attention on God's plan for MAN rather than for the rest of creation. Because it was born in times of terrible stress, times when the end of the world was indeed widely expected, it has tended to put its hopes on the next world rather than on the present one. And even when that expectation lapsed, Christian thought always feared the dilution of monotheism by nature-worship. It has therefore often sharply discouraged direct concern for the natural world. Thus, both St Augustine and St Thomas Aquinas ruled that any idea that we could have a duty to animals was unchristian. Similarly Charlemagne, when he christianized his subjects, required just one test of their genuine conversion – namely, that they were now willing to cut down trees. And this kind of attitude has remained traditional among many orthodox Christian authorities. It is apparently still shared today by Pope John Paul II.

But there is a quite different strand in the Judaeo-Christian tradition which vigorously celebrates the whole of creation as equally God's work. This strand is certainly stronger in the Old than in the New Testament, but it has always been recognised as an essential part of doctrine. And in the last two centuries it has steadily gained ground. Serious Christian writers today find no difficulty in accommodating the environmental message. Aberrations like the apocalyptic fundamentalism that I mentioned earlier stand apart from thoughtful Christianity.

This reverence for nature as God's creation was, too, the starting point from which the great Romantic poets – Goethe, Coleridge, Wordsworth, Blake – launched a new and deeper recognition of it. They did not just celebrate the power and beauty of non-human nature. They also made possible a world-vision which showed human beings as a part of it rather than as detached observers over against it. They stressed our continuity with the rest of the physical world rather than our separation from it. They pioneered a reverent, accepting stance rather than a hostile, defensive or contemptuous one towards that world, and they rightly saw that stance as perfectly compatible with Christian thinking.

Today, in any case, this ambivalent role of Christianity is the less important half of our story. Far more influential among decision-makers now are political ideas derived from the Enlightenment and eventually from the Greeks, notably individualism, the social contract and the Rights of Man. The political struggles which forged those ideas were struggles against human oppression, against the tyranny of governments. Their ruling ideal was quite simply human freedom. Both those people on the Left who called for Liberty, Equality and Fraternity and those people on the Right who demanded commercial freedom were asserting the rights of one set of human beings against another.

In this drama, the rest of nature plays no role.

Concern for plants and animals tends to be dismissed, very much as St Thomas dismissed it, as a superstitious distraction from the only objective that really matters, namely, the prosperity of MAN. By and large, many people in our culture see the Enlightenment message simply as proving that human self-interest is the only rational motive. Indeed, they often assume that this self-interest *defines* rationality, as many economists still take it to do.

Can We Start Again From Scratch?

So it would no doubt be possible today for environmentalists who attend only to this familiar propaganda to dismiss the Enlightenment, equally with Christianity, as providing no grounds for taking non-human nature seriously and so to call (as some of them do) for an entirely new ethic, purpose-built and designed from scratch. New ethics, however, cannot be thus built. They are not put together like Lego castles, nor are they bought like new hats. They are much more ecological than that. Like ecosystems, they have to grow. Indeed, they are a part of that very dense ecosystem, our existing communal life, and they have to grow out of the plants and soil that are already there. The idea of an approach so 'post-modern' that it uses no earlier ideas is mere self-deception. Doctrines which claim this sort of novelty actually display their ancestry as clearly as any others.

There are in fact plenty of materials available. The reductive, dismissive attitude to nature that I have just described was only one possible form of the Enlightenment message and by no means the central one. The greatest prophets of the Age of Reason certainly did not share it. Rousseau spoke up powerfully for the whole of non-human nature. Voltaire, Tom Paine, Bentham and John Stuart Mill all sharply attacked the ill-treatment of animals. The idea of the Rights of Man was certainly not meant originally to be a way of devaluing everything non-human but simply a way of demanding concern for all humans. These people had enough largeness of spirit to see beyond human squabbles to the wider context of life.

It is true that this more generous, humanitarian attitude to other species does not mesh easily with the more formal, legalistic language which surrounds the notion of *rights*. There is an implicit conflict here between two main parts of Enlightenment morality – humanitarianism and legalism - a conflict which is still making trouble over a number of issues (including the notion of 'animal rights') today. No doubt, too, the partisan opposition of most Enlightenment sages to religion gave them a slant which did limit their imaginative grasp, and which defines the Enlightenment as constituting only one side of our recent tradition. But this limitation promptly generated its own response in the counter-movement that we loosely call the Romantic Revival. Our tradition already contains plenty of ideas that can enable us to resist narrow-minded self-worship. If we want material, it is there. Why can't we use it?

Trouble Over Progress

The reason lies, I think, chiefly in the still dominant nineteenth-century conception of progress and especially in the form given to it by Social Darwinism. The idea that human intellectual and technological progress are the leading edge of a predestined wider upward movement, a movement which constitutes the purpose of the entire cosmos and is bound to go on into the indefinite future, makes it very hard to take any other world-picture seriously.

This idea of cosmic progress, first fully formulated by Darwin's contemporary, Herbert Spencer, caught on very strongly during the early Industrial Revolution. Though the worship of the human intellect that underlies it has often been attacked, this picture has not really been shifted from its role as a guiding and consoling vision. It serves to replace the long-term guarantees that were previously offered by religion, while still paying lip-service to science.

In order to provide this lip-service, the cosmic progress is now usually called 'evolution' This name was invented by the French naturalist J-B.Lamarck and used by Spencer. Darwin, distrusting its euphoric implications, did not use it. Rather confidingly, however, today's biologists do use it, thus sometimes giving the quite misleading impression that modern biology validates Lamarck's concept of predestined progress. In fact 'evolution' as modern biologists understand it is something quite different. It is not a movement with a single direction at all, and it gives no kind of special importance to the human species. It is what Darwin called it, simply – 'the modification of species' – all species – in various piecemeal directions by their various environments. It is a bush-like process of development with no up or down, no given terminus to aim at, and certainly no guaranteed future.

Spencer's non-scientific, anti-Darwinian notion of evolution is, however, at present freely celebrated in best-selling, apparently scientific books written by eminent cosmologists. This is not just a harmless aberration. It matters because it introduces radical confusion into contemporary notions of the relations between science and religion. It offers faith in what is actually a gratuitous fancy as something endorsed by science. There is also, however, a political point of even graver concern about the mechanism by which progress is supposed to work.

Spencer and his 'Social Darwinist' followers conceived their upward progress as driven by egoistic competition between individual beings at all levels. Projecting the euphoria of raw, emergent nineteenth-century capitalism onto a cosmic scale, they saw individual selfishness as the engine running the whole advance. They wholly neglected the deeper and more central role of co-operation, which is always necessary before any competition can take place at all. This Spencerian myth is what still underlies the exclusive reliance on the concept of selfishness in popular books like *The Selfish Gene* and in the other literature of Sociobiology.

In human life, the superficiality of this Social Darwinist psychology has often been exposed. Reappearing, however, at this mysterious cosmic level and with apparent scientific backing, it has gained renewed prestige. It is, of course, a conception that seems to justify fully the species-selfishness of the prototypically rational creatures that are supposed to be heading the sublime process towards hyperintelligence – ourselves. And in an increasingly frightening age, such long-term hopes are not easily abandoned. Thus, our civilization's current march towards planetary suicide is now sustained and heartened by bizarre hopes of eternal cosmic dominion.

Conclusion

That, I suggest, is the vision that we need to attack. Visions, however, can only be countered by other visions. Arguments alone do not touch them. But arguments that convey a vision can be a very good lever for shifting them.

This is the kind of lever that Lovelock offers, and it is extremely important that literal-minded people should not reject his vision simply because it is distinct from his detailed arguments. Both components are needed and both belong together.

We need every kind of picture that can put back some balance into our imaginative life, breaking the current crazy idea that competition is prudent and is indeed the only possible reality. Since benign visions command less attention than sinister ones, how about supplementing Lovelock's image by considering once more the history of Easter Island?

What we most need to know of that story is retold well and clearly by Clive Ponting in his book *A Green History of the World*. This small and very remote island in the South Pacific is, of course, known to us chiefly because of its statues. From the early eighteenth century, Western explorers who happened on the place stood stunned and speechless by these colossal stone male heads and torsos. More than six hundred of them are set up on more than fifty platforms – platforms which are themselves skilfully built from large stone blocks. Some of the platforms have sophisticated astronomical alignments, usually towards the solstices or the equinox. Many of the statues have been knocked over but many still stand. Their average height is twenty feet but one of them tops sixty-nine feet – the height of a seven-story building.

Latter-day natives of the island are, however, few, depressed and unprosperous. Living near subsistence level, they are obviously incapable of such grand works. So early travellers supposed that the sublime architects must have come from some more prestigious civilization. But this still did not explain the extraordinary haste with which the work had been abandoned. More than half the statues are still standing or lying at all angles in the quarry where they were made. (This quarry is about ten miles from their destined platforms.) Some of these have just been started, some are nearly finished, some are complete but awaiting transport. Some, too, have been dropped half-way to their destination.

Everywhere there are signs of a sudden, hasty interruption. Tools, casually dropped, lie about everywhere in the quarry. And these tools are all of stone. Evidently the work was indeed all done by its native inhabitants, done by patient chipping with stone picks. There is no metal on the island. Neither are there, now, any trees there except for a few in remote volcanic craters. The place is infertile and only just supports its present small population. How did it ever feed and fuel the huge numbers needed for these works?

Archaeologists have found the melancholy answer to this question. Pollen analysis shows that the island was once covered with dense vegetation, including plentiful woods. But during the thousand years after AD 500, when people first came there, the growing population began to wear down these resources. The last straw, however, was unmistakably the statue industry. Transporting and setting up the colossi required an enormous amount of timber for roads and scaffolding. The various clans, competing hotly to outdo each other's ceremonial terraces, worked on without stint until they had used up all available trees for that purpose.

About 1600, accordingly, the island became completely deforested. That was when statue-building came to a sudden stop. And the rest of life changed too. With no wood left for houses, people took to living in flimsy reed huts or shelters dug into the hillsides. Without proper material for nets, they had trouble in fishing. The fertile soil, without trees to bind it, began to leach away. But more serious still, these various shortages, together with the previous competitive culture, quickly led to bitter and chronic civil war, a war in which many of the statues were overthrown. Nor could those who disliked this situation leave the island because – without trees – there was no possible way of making canoes in which to do so.

As Clive Ponting points out, this disaster cannot have been only a material one for the Easter Islanders:

> The social and cultural impact of deforestation was equally important. The inability to erect any more statues must have had a devastating effect on the belief systems and social organisation and called into question the foundations on which that complex society had been built . . . Slavery became common and, as the amount of protein available fell, the population turned to cannibalism . . .

And so forth. What astonishes us – each time that we hear of it – is the way in which such obviously approaching shortages don't inhibit building. Traces of this same obsessive process have been seen in many ruined cities elsewhere, especially in that cradle of human civilization, the Near East. People occupied in constructing something grand are extremely slow to see that they might need to worry about the ground that they stand on and the air that they are breathing. The statues were evidently the Easter Islanders' skyscrapers, their Empire State Building, their moonshot and Tokyo Tower and Canary Wharf. Or, as Shelley more neatly put it,

> I met a traveller from an antique land
> Who said; Two vast and trunkless legs of stone
> Stand in the desert . . .

And on the pedestal these words appear;
'My name is Ozymandias, king of kings,
Look on my works, ye Mighty, and despair!'
Nothing beside remains. Round the decay
Of that colossal wreck, boundless and bare
The lone and level sands stretch far away.

Oscar Moore

Fatality Rites

> He swears every now and then to begin a better life.
> But when night comes with its own counsel,
> its own compromises and prospects –
> when night comes with its own power
> of a body that needs and demands,
> he returns, lost, to the same fatal pleasure.
>
> *He Swears*, C.P. Cavafy

Even before it had started, we knew. Even before anyone had whispered words like fatal in the same breath as pleasure, we had guessed.

> Everyone was at it. Dancing, sweating, smoking, steaming. Handkerchiefs soaked in ethyl chloride were crammed in people's mouths, or hung from head to head like laundry lines across the dance floor, each mouth taking a corner. And as Hugo watched the dizzy heads above the naked torsos, big from pumping

> iron, ready for the big night in the big noise club, a thought passed quietly through his head. That maybe this was the end. The last dance on the *Titanic*. The last squelch of a Roman debauchery. The last rites of a demented sect. The end.
> (*A Matter of Life and Sex*, Oscar Moore)

By the time I came to write *A Matter of Life and Sex* in London between 1985 and 1989, I already knew what was happening in the gay communities of London and New York, Los Angeles and San Francisco, among the drug-users of Amsterdam, Paris and Rome and along the highways of central Africa (although, like most, I was less aware of the depth of the African crisis). But my novel was set in a real time, before the wave of panic and its surf (or scurf) of moral hysteria had crashed over our heads. Amid a lot of the fictional elisions and inventions of my novel, this was a real memory of an actual moment at Heaven one Saturday night in about 1981. And my Hugo Harvey, smoking, dancing and fucking in London, was not alone. On the other side of the Atlantic, in New York's notorious Mineshaft, another Englishman was experiencing (and then, like Hugo, ignoring) the same shudders of apprehension. 'I had never seen anything like it: fist-fucking, racks and the stench of piss and poppers and everything else and the heat and the men and the light was all red and I remembered thinking, standing there, adrenalin thundering around me, "This is evil, this is wrong."' Rupert Haselden talking to Simon Garfield in *The End of Innocence*.

At the time, these shudders within the gay community were rooted more in physical queasiness than any moral qualms. Morality was the language and preserve of the establishment. With the naming of AIDS came a legion of politicians and journalists eager to wrap the emerging dead in flags of their convenience. The press routinely described haemophiliacs, the non-sexual victims, as innocent, so that those who had been infected in the course of sexual and narcotic indulgence were by implication guilty. While this sexy morality may have sold newspapers it, perhaps not surprisingly, failed to change our sexual mores. Instead of being converted (presumably into born-again heterosexuals or at least celibates) we became entrenched, barricaded against their barracking. But as we hardened our faces against Fleet Street's snickering prurience we had little energy left for introspection and self-analysis. The media viewed the emerging crisis through the stained glass window of their neo-Victorian Thatcherite pieties, while we, furious at their warped perspective, stared at ourselves from behind rose-tinted mirror shades.

What we did sense, however, and what is summed up in Cavafy's 'fatal pleasure', was that something was going to give. It was a fear that owed more to the laws of physics than to the conventions of morality; what goes up must come down. (Of course, physiology also obtains: whatever you take to keep it up can leave you feeling very down, as any experienced user of amyl nitrite will admit.) Just as every action creates a reaction, so every indulgence carries its consequence as surely as the party brings its hangover. But this tension between pleasure and pain went deeper than the relationship between a drink and a headache.

From the serpent and the apple to George Bataille's image of orgasm as 'a little death', sex and sexual knowledge have always been inextricably bound in an embrace with death. And for most of the previous centuries that death required little imagination. Syphilis and gonorrhœa were killers before the panacea of penicillin, a cushion of security and comfort that was only two generations old. Old enough for us to have forgotten the truth of the embrace, but too recent for the atavistic resonance of the ancient intermingling of sex and death, pleasure and pain to have been erased. And before the religiose start their diatribes against the extra-marital and casual, not to mention homosexual, sex, childbirth should be added to the list of killers.

The irony was that here, in the late seventies and early eighties, we, the modern, sophisticated, cosmopolitan and emancipated, were stuck on the ancient seesaw of pleasure and pain. We had been high for so long that we had to come down. Of course it hadn't really been so long. The generation before us had lived furtive lives of secrecy and gloom. Appropriately, their greatest freedoms had been enjoyed during the blackout (often in the company of Americans). But while a few still found an erotic charge in the habits of concealment and coded communication, the emancipation and enlightenment of the sixties and seventies had propelled us to new heights of social prominence and sexual promiscuity. The heights may have left us giddy, but we were having too much fun to want to come down. And yet come down we would. We had been partying so hard the hangover had to be harder. For that moment, however, we couldn't see it coming. After all, there was nothing in our lifetime's experience of medicine to prepare us for the attack . . . or was there?

Within our belief in the dogma of progress was a faith in medicine as the cure rather than the palliative. Despite the occasional sceptical voice – notably Anthony Clare's in the *Listener*, who, writing one of his regular columns in the early eighties, detailed the continuing havoc wreaked by more than twenty fatal and incurable diseases from rheumatoid arthritis to multiple sclerosis, and emphasised how cures were lucky breaks rather than dependable events – like all good citizens of the post-war west, we believed firmly in the delivery of relief via prescription with a guarantee of healthy recuperation appended.

But our conviction that medical progress was a simple, regular and linear ascent was about to be destroyed by new strains of home-grown diseases and the unexpected arrival of new violent and sociopathic illnesses which seemed to have emigrated from distant environments by that most modern of medical transmitters, the aeroplane. Not that we were naive about sexual diseases. We knew the hazards. We were all veterans of the STD clinics. The clap was something you knocked back with a week's dose of Penbritin. Crabs could be washed away with Ascabia, even if the sight of the little mites flexing their legs in desperation as you plucked them from your pubic hair made you nauseous. And we knew about pain. For syphilis, the penicillin had to be administered by syringe into your buttock muscle, a treacle of medication that left you scarcely able to sit or smile for the rest of the day. In fact, for about half an hour after the injection, all you could do was lie down and wait for the pain to ebb and then you had to spend the rest of the day finding plausible explanations as to why you couldn't sit without a grimace and why you took every step with caution. Imagine being reduced to inventing haemorrhoids as a cover. And despite the carefully hushed voices of the social workers gathered to counsel you before you left the clinic's clutches, you knew that this was no longer a medically fatal disease, just a socially irksome one.

But things were changing and the mutterings were spreading. There were some new viruses on the block – infections that seemed to cause a lot more damage and others that didn't seem to want to go away. There was hepatitis, which came in a whole alphabet soup of variations, one of which could keep you in bed for six months, terrified of alcohol and jaundiced like a sallow skeleton. There was herpes, which wouldn't go away at all. Of course, at the time, this didn't seem to be our problem. It was the girls – the real ones who actually wore dresses and had real tits – who suffered from it. We would watch them arriving for an appointment at the STD clinic, sitting in physical pain and social shame amid the *Tatler*s and *Country Life*s of the waiting room, sometimes with, sometimes without their carrier-male wearing his guilt chain round a hung head. And we would drop our eyes and smile inwardly at their distress, just like the veterans of the piste laughing at the beginners as they stumbled on the nursery slopes. We didn't know yet then that other herpes viruses such as zoster (shingles) would be one of the key marker diseases of AIDS and that cytomegalovirus – benign in the rest of the population – would end up eating our retinas and leaving us blind.

Even the old faithfuls were behaving oddly. There was talk of a new strain of the clap that wouldn't go away. And now there was something doing the rounds in New York which left visible marks, so people could see that you were sick. That could really screw up your cruising! They said it was some kind of skin cancer, apparently, and that maybe it came from poppers. Maybe you should stop using poppers. But then how were you going to get fucked? And anyway sex just wasn't the same without the drugs. Poppers made sex intense, although sometimes a little too brief. And afterwards your head hurt much too much to make conversation. But fucking was literally a pain in the ass otherwise. So they destroyed the art of sexual small-talk, along with half a lobe of brain cells, but sex without them would be like being banished to the paddling pool after sampling the pleasures of the hot tub (we hadn't quite figured out that it was the pleasures of the hot tub that had got us into the hot water in the first place).

But the suggestion that we were in some way inviting infection through our habits and that the retinue of regular afflictions we routinely suffered boded ill was one that provoked fury and rebuke, with gay spokesmen alleging that the threat of illness was being used as a cover for the return of long-held and only recently challenged sexual prejudices. This was after all the era of Clause 28. And if the doubts were expressed by one of our own, we turned on him just as viciously. When Rupert Haselden wrote in the *Guardian*, in a piece entitled 'Gay Abandon', of the 'inbuilt fatalism of being gay', and described the self-indulgent and self-destructive behaviour of gay men as a consequence of our being 'biologically maladaptive, unable to reproduce . . . [and] without offspring to make sense of life', he touched a raw nerve. The subsequent demonstrations outside the offices of the *Guardian* and the public declarations of contempt from gay figures did not disguise the reality of the anxieties that Haselden had uncovered. It was the pointed probing of our social and political anxieties that echoed in the shrill denials. His view of the emotional emptiness of a life without children, bent upon itself and the pursuit of pleasure in the night world's hall of mirrors, reflecting the acquired images of a thousand narcissi, is still virulently denied. But while it is easy for a gay man to idealise the family without remembering the sacrifices required to start one (interestingly, many heterosexuals of the yuppie era also seem to have decided that their life is too good to spoil) and the tensions of surviving within one, the anger Haselden's article provoked was tinny with self-justification and unease.

And yet Haselden knew what he was talking about. He had been there. In truth we all knew, but we carried on, fiddling with each other while Rome burned . . . or smouldered. We turned a blind eye in a brave face . . . for as long as we could. But by 1983 it was getting too hard to ignore. The bath-houses were still open – not least because of the unlikely coalition of straight owners and their gay clientele against the advice and efforts of the health authorities. But the faces along the dimly lit corridors were showing tensions, anxieties and even the occasional lesion.

By that summer, men who knew themselves to be sick were still luring partners into their clutches, and those partners, with the help of a line, a toke and a whiff were throwing off caution with their towels. Not everyone had a mission, but in some ways Gaetan Dugas, the infamous Patient Zero who, having become one of the first people to be diagnosed HIV positive (hence his statistical appellation), then decided to take as many down with him as he could, was the evil mascot of this era, and not simply because of his sexual vendetta.

That in itself was a potent enough image: the beautiful ruined 'boy', furious at the onset of debilitating (and looks-diminishing) decay, livid that he should have become a victim when for so long he had been the queen, taking his revenge for the 'unfairness' of his fate by secretly poisoning his lovers with his sperm. If anyone defined the flimsiness of gay solidarity it was Dugas. But the Air Canada airline steward who criss-crossed the USA from gay metropolis to bath-house resort, was also symptomatic of a key catalyst in the spread of the virus.

While the transmission of the virus from one partner to the other required the mingling and exchange of blood – hence the particular vulnerability of the passive 'fuckee' (anal sex often involving some bleeding), intravenous drug users and haemophiliacs requiring regular infusions of blood-clotting agents – it is not too fanciful to think HIV relied equally on airborne delivery via cheap transatlantic airtravel to make its most significant journey.

The role of Skytrain in the spread of AIDS is a socio-economic document yet to be written, but for twenty-year-old students like myself, looking at long vac options on a low budget, the downward plunge in transatlantic fares triggered by Freddie Laker was the mechanical catalyst required to take me from London to New York for my date with the bug.

Like hundreds, maybe thousands, of sexual tourists, I travelled the gay transatlantic free (or at least very cheap) way every summer for four years.

It is arguable that it was the same cheap air travel that was required to take a virus from central Africa into Manhattan, San Francisco, LA. This may be fanciful. Randy Shilts in his seminal history of the disease, *And the Band Played On*, uses the occasion of the American Bicentennial, and the arrival of the tall ships in New York from all over the globe, as the moment when an invisible alien may have disembarked. His image is more symbolically accurate than medically certain. But whatever mode of transport it chose for that first transatlantic crossing, the history of a virus, which had lain dormant in its host species in central Africa for possible millennia, is intimately involved with the changes in human movement. While the occasional missionary, doctor and aid worker went down in an isolated and still mysterious case, often returning to home and baffled hospital staff to die, and while one of the first supposed cases was reported (although at that stage neither named nor understood) in a merchant seaman who died in Manchester in 1959, the virus at that stage was still travelling by slow boat and landing on stony ground.

What it needed was jet travel and a hot tub at the other end, although the spread of the disease in central Africa and now in Brazil has depended on another transport conduit: the highways used by truckers and the prostitutes who service them. What it also needed was gay men who said fuck fate, let's fuck. And we did. But underneath the bravado, beneath the narcotic veneer and the alcohol sweat, we were getting anxious. The smallest things suddenly seemed terrifyingly significant: an unseasonal cold, an unexplained cough and, worst of all, a strange skin rash.

March 1983: my diary, New York City, the Weekend (26-27 March)
Something of an epic which has left me with an unsightly, neurosis-inducing rash at the top of my chest . . . I pray for deliverance.

Got back to 97th Street at about 2pm. Had a bath, etc, and then Adam and I went down to the Park. Had a couple of joints with John, a friend of Ralph's who runs an ice-cream stand in the Park. Then, by now completely smashed, we wandered round the Park in the sunshine, babbling, giggling, analysing and giggling.

Back to 97th Street and then, after a quick meal, down to cocaine-Jaime's in the East Village. Went with him and his dull nephew and his wife to see Carlos Montoya at the Carnegie Hall but I was so stoned I slept through most of it.

Met up with ice-cream John and his boyfriend Frankie, and we eventually headed off to The Saint. Took a couple of ups, a Peach melba tab, and Jaime was very generous with the cocaine. I danced a lot, had a lot of sex – took mad risks in the 'fuck room' balcony by fucking a total stranger (three times, but at least it was the same one each time). Got a surprise blow-job from ice-cream John (I learned later that both he and Frankie have the hots for me). We left The Saint at 12 noon on Sunday, and the three of us – Adam, Ralph and I – went down to the St Mark's Baths for a swim and sauna, etc. More light relief followed and we stumbled out into the rain at 6pm on Sunday, had a Chinese meal and passed out.

Met the most gorgeous blond hunk, Karl, at the Baths, but at that stage I was too shattered to perform and Ralph and Adam wanted to leave. Took his number and promised to call him on my return from Washington. There are two problems – this rash, and he is into fist-fucking, which makes him a heavy risk area as far as AIDS is concerned. But the rash I think is drugs not sex.

I don't know what happened to Karl. Adam is dead. Ralph was dying when Adam left New York for Sydney in 1984, already freaked by the havoc around him as hospitals choked on gay cases and insurance companies scribbled new exclusion clauses.

Karl, with whom I spent a coke-fuelled teeth-clenching night of passionless sex, was one of those good-looking Europeans kept by a rich American in a scarcely furnished mid-town apartment (huge empty expanses of parquet, picture-less walls and curtain-less windows were always tell-tale coke signs). If he didn't die of cocaine abuse – we did more that night than my chest and brain could bear and it took me most of the next day to come down on hashish parachutes – then he may well have died of AIDS. We had frequent unprotected sex that night. Somehow mentioning condoms implied sickness not caution. There was a fragile conspiracy of silence and pretence that could not be broken without cracking the erotic aura. To mention a rubber was to rub out passion. But I am convinced that that rash was my 'conversion trauma'.

Returning to England was hardly a comfort. By now the press were picking up the story of the 'Gay Plague', and indulging the prejudices of a readership that liked a lurid mixture of voyeurism and morality – peeking and preaching. The tabloids stirred their stories with a generous dose of fake hysteria and acquired outrage, which left us in a state of siege (hence our Custer-style last stand over the bath-houses). 'Fleet Street does not like homosexuality', said Derek Jameson, then editor of the *Daily Star*, on a BBC Open Space programme and suddenly it seemed as if no one did. We had gone from the envied social butterflies of an international fashion, music, nightclub trail to the moths singed in our own candle as we burnt it at every end. The rudest shock was to discover that for all our well-placed 'sisters' we had no political clout, no voice in the corridors of power. Any who made it into those carpeted cloisters immediately went into asexual mufti. The loud and declared were banging on a closed door, the same closed door behind which some of the best potential allies and most dangerous enemies remained closeted. Even Peter Tatchell, now the virulent mouth on endless rally platforms, ducked the issue of whom he fucked while trying to win a traditional Labour constituency in the Isle of Dogs.

This was not a time to come out and for many of us the rising tide of homophobia – even leading to suggestions of island encampments for the perverted and the diseased, notions redolent of Nazism – was not simply a media aberration. Gay-bashing suddenly seemed to have an unspoken sanction, and emerging from Heaven into Villiers Street in the early hours of the morning, one was watchful and wary, tucking any instantly recognisable gay garb into bags and keeping head down, baseball cap on, collar up and voice low.

In these, the middle years of the eighties and the incubator years of the illness, the press played to the gallery, to the same sniggering onlookers who used to laugh at the trials of men caught cottaging in the West End and taken to task at Bow Street Magistrates Court. 'AIDS is like everything else,' wrote a *Sun* reader. 'When you mess up with nature you have it coming to you, mate. Homosexuality isn't natural. And if it isn't natural, it goes against the laws of nature. It's just another plague.'

This was frightening stuff. The mood of the nation had turned on us like a poisonous tide. We had gone from being the envied and even desired, to the mocked and repudiated and we weren't even getting sick yet. Amid all this tabloid morality-du-jour, one article in particular seemed to chill more deeply. Reviewing the Horizon programme, 'Killer in the Village', for the *Observer* (11 May 1983), Martin Amis listed the 'eerie invitation to disease' that AIDS presented, stressing how these illnesses were something new, something odd. 'Brain diseases carried by cats, types of TB carried by birds, profound diarrhoea carried by livestock: AIDS is a visitation that makes you believe in the devil.'

It was as if we had been caught in an early edition of the 'X-files' or 'Tales of the Unexpected'. How could we be expected to remain calm when we were facing such an Hitchcockian onslaught? And Amis' invocation of the devil tapped a whole other anxiety. While the politicians were ignoring us, the Christians, exhibiting that charity for which they are so known, were denouncing us. The Anglican Church tried to be warm and caring, and the Catholic Church stayed quiet, relying on the bombastic authoritarianism of the Pope to cover up the panic in the cloisters, but the evangelists called on us to repent and rent our hems (no matter what designer label), presumably before diseases of cats and dogs were joined by a rain of the animals themselves.

It was a tense time, and we clung to our moments of defiant irony (my favourite being Jimmy Somerville's cover version of Donna Summer's 'I Feel Love', recorded not long after the singing diva's religiose pronouncements on damned perverts had led to mass smashings of her records at gay meetings across the States).

But, by now, the realisation that we were politically impotent and sexually isolated was giving way to the more personal panic as people we knew began to get sick.

I lost my first two friends to AIDS in 1989, two years after I confirmed that the rash in New York of 1983 was indeed a signal of my 'conversion'. I can remember the freeze in my veins when one friend rang me on holiday, to say that the decorating job he had started for me while I was away would not be finished when I came back because he had been taken to hospital with severe headaches. He joked about hoarding DF118s. But he never recovered. I can remember my cold sweats in the lift at Westminster Hospital, having been sitting by the end of a wizened and shrivelled friend emaciated by diarrhoea and racked with strange pains. All the time one thought kept echoing in the background like an infernal chorus: 'You're next. Just you wait. You'll be here.'

It became harder and harder to visit sick friends as they became less and less able to mask their bitterness, desolation and fear. I remember arriving at the house of a former flatmate one day, half an hour later than I had planned and promised to. He was blinded by CMV retinitis, emaciated by diarrhoea and tortured by headaches but still had the breath to berate me for talking about the traffic on my journey to see him. 'What the fuck do I care about traffic?' he gasped. 'Shut up and roll a joint.' I did, and then in a sudden swoon of nausea retreated to the bathroom and almost dissolved in a drenching flop-sweat.

But while we had discovered the true depth of our isolation – from the politicians, from the pundits, from the opinion formers and their echo chambers – we had discovered one incredible ally: the National Health Service. To begin with the relationship was tentative, but that was more to do with nervousness than hostility. In the mid-eighties it was hard to get a test, no matter how high risk you could prove yourself to be, partly because the inevitability of the progression from HIV to AIDS was not yet established, and partly because doctors were unable to cope with the fall-out: the despair, panic and occasionally the suicides of people diagnosed positive, given a short plank to a grim plunge. I remember trying to explain to a very considerate but unyielding doctor at my regular STD clinic that, as a one-time intravenous-drug-using homosexual with a history of frequent trips to New York bath-houses, a taste for multiple, often simultaneous, partners and an appetite for narcotics of most flavours, I was my own walking red alert. Still he refused to test me and I ended up going to the kind of IN/OUT Harley Street affair, from where the results were sent direct to my GP, thereby leaving me with a future of insurance policy nightmares. Scenarios like these only added to the fears and anxieties surrounding the whole issue of being tested: was having the test an act of sexual responsibility or an invitation to instant social, professional and financial death and a plunge into the ice-bath of personal paranoia? Was ignorance not just a thin version of bliss but an equally flimsy last defence against ostracism and isolation? For a time it appeared as if we had no one to turn to but ourselves . . . and we were all too scared to talk about it.

But, as the decade and the disease progressed, our relationship with the NHS became intimate, positive and a crucial safety net. For an illness that had such multiple manifestations it was necessary to fight on every front: as urgent as developing eventual cures and current palliatives via patient trials was the need to maintain general health and fitness through dietary vigilance and supplements. Traditional Chinese herbs and over-the-counter vitamins became an intrinsic part of a pharmacological armoury that included, at the sharp (although often disappointingly blunt) end, the latest trial drugs from the laboratories of Glaxo Wellcome or Hoffman La Roche. AIDS victims and the HIV positive became active partners with their doctors in a series of experiments and trials, and the information on the potentials of each new drug was mediated through a growing brace of support groups and newsletters.

Of course life can easily become a ghost train of phantom anxieties, shuttling no longer between office and home but between ward and waiting room, troubled by trying to assess whether a headache is the result of a long drink and a short sleep, or the onset of toxoplasmosis, whether a chest pain is due to one too many cigarettes or a return of pleurisy, and whether an upward surge of gas means that *Candida* is surging down your oesophagus or food that didn't agree with you. Meanwhile some anxieties are becoming disturbingly real: in particular the return to the funding crisis.

For the last six years I have enjoyed the luxury of being a research priority with ring-fenced funding, demarcated beds, underwritten prescriptions. I, and hundreds of others, have lived on the medical fast-track, enjoying a rare two-way dialogue with doctors, research nurses and consultants eager to partner their patients in investigating an illness that had to be fought on so many fronts that all and any weapons were welcome. But now, as the rate of increase fails to increase as projected (which of course just means that the incidence of the illness is rising at the same rate every year) we are threatened with budget cuts, lost beds, and a loss of the special care and attention that made hospital wards like the Middlesex's Broderip Ward, where I spent a total of five months in 1994, a sanctuary of calm and care. Of course in some ways this is medical science being a victim of its own success. As AIDS sufferers survive longer, thanks to improved care and successful prophylactics, existing cases are costing more. I myself have already outlived several predictions of imminent death, and my demand for new treatments places further burden on an already stretched budget.

And this in a context of broadening demographics. AIDS is no longer a possession of the gay community, and ironically it is one we are finding hard to relinquish. It turned a fragmented population of sexual opportunists into a community of mutual aid. It gave us a cause for which to fight and we managed to convert fear and loathing into respect, admiration and collaboration. We created charities that are now the semi-official organs of government policy and we cultivated a new sense of responsibility among the previously mocking or antagonistic media, which meant that the recent release of the Delta Trial results, regarding the success of combination therapy involving AZT, DDC and DDI, was covered by leading national newspapers and *all* the major news services.

Perhaps nurtured by these partnerships, and certainly informed by them, a sense of community began to emerge within the gay world. In the late seventies and early eighties, the word 'community' seemed an exaggeratedly optimistic term for what was little more than a series of interlinking casual fucks and a variety of predatory gatherings across town. There were publications, guides, travel organisations and, of course, bars, restaurants and even cinemas, but they all seemed principally devoted to the business of introducing prospective sexual partners: and if you weren't either well-built or well-heeled you could find yourself languishing in the unwelcome company of the unwanted. But by the mid-eighties the community, united in crisis, began to deserve the name. Galvanised, it organised and petitioned, emerging as a sophisticated and effective lobbying force (after all, a large proportion of its 'members' had worked in the media for years). For the first time we seemed to have established a dialogue with politicians, relationships with television and newspapers, and, crucially, an effective and vital service within our own community delivering help, companionship, food and information.

Inevitably divisions remain. The political and social image of Crusaid, compared to the Terrence Higgins Trust or Gay Men Fighting Aids, is almost diametrically opposed and a certain amount of cross-fire can be heard backfiring from the media barricades every time all three are called to comment. But the issue is not one of the conflicts between them, but of their collective ability to embrace a broad church, from the politically aggressive to the financially affluent from the red flag to the pink pound.

And if we have knitted affinities among ourselves, we have also constructed bridges to the outside world. The gay community's battle with AIDS won it an audience and, later, a respect that was a new experience after years of indifference and mockery. At the simplest level, there was an acknowledgement of the quiet dignity of the collective struggle in the face of a peculiarly versatile and elusive enemy. And, at the more public level, there was the realisation, as the death rolls were read out and published in ever increasing length, of the breadth, depth and weight of gay culture.

It has been a long journey from the secret suffering of Rock Hudson, but now as cutbacks and reorganisations threaten the autonomy and efficiency of the country's leading AIDS units, we are also having to face the fact that like so many other more frivolous things that we started, this is a disease that has crossed over. It is increasingly part of a larger picture. As the gay community got smart, active and vigilant, the spread of the disease moved to new demographics – but the reputation and name, the 'Gay Plague', was always a distortion. New and growing communities of sufferers are increasingly visible here, but the massive tragedy is of course in the parts of the world neglected by news crews and newspapers. It is bitterly ironic that the source of this and other newly emergent viruses - the central African rainforest – remains a small item in a side-column in most national newspapers. Just as the local demographics of the disease broaden and diverge, so does the sinister fraternity of new viruses. While the evangelical want to see in AIDS a retribution for our corrupt morality, the truth is that HIV is only one of many emergent viruses, awakened from dormancy, released from their host species and playing havoc with our sense of medical security. The Health Transition programmes of the sixties now seem oddly naive, notwithstanding their real successes, as a plethora of new and deadly viruses has taken advantage of the same conduit of international travel, 'liberated' by local agricultural and geological disruption, to launch themselves on an unsuspecting humanity.

The guerrilla insurgents of the Vietcong, destroying a huge imperialist foe from tiny military cells, seem now part of a military anachronism as the new insurgents carry names like Ebola, Lassa and Hanta, and organise their cell activity from within the body of the victim, in their own sinister version of colonisation. In this context, HIV loses its edge as the evangelical finger of retribution. It is part of a larger biochemical battle between the human species and its environment, and whatever its horrors it has been upstaged by the savage deaths of haemorrhagic fevers (Ebola).

Neither are all the foes new ones with tropical names and distant homes. The emergence of antibiotic-resistant strains of once vanquished diseases – particularly tuberculosis, which now lurks in a deadly, untreatable form in at least one medical faculty freezer – tilts our whole notion of human progress and superiority. Are these the new barbarians and Visigoths, standing by at the fall of our Rome?

The hysteria takes a small spark to reignite: recent outbreaks of meningitis have achieved immediate national coverage and calls for calm and restraint. But with historical precedents like the Black Death – a holocaust more profound than any world war that destroyed 75 per cent of the known population of the world and was itself triggered by sudden changes in the migratory habits of the species (this time the Mongol hordes) – such speculation seems less melodramatic.

Our frontline remains at home, on the ward, in the clinic and in the political and domestic chamber. There are many new challenges to be won: as the government cuts health budgets and starts to reintegrate AIDS care into general medicine and genito-urinary departments, researchers, specialists and funding will be lost, not because the battle has been won but because the rate of increase is not increasing. But unless vigilance is maintained, that statistic will also soon be untrue.

Already it appears that AIDS has developed its own generation gap. After spending the mid-eighties in the ice-bucket of fear, the national gay libido re-emerged in the nineties determined to have fun. New clubs chose names that defiantly declared a return to sex and sexuality: Love Muscle, Adonis Lounge, Trade. While it would be dangerous to counteract this flourishing of a dormant sexual energy with the tactics of paranoia, every generation represents its own educational challenge. Personally, my experience of living with AIDS, although occasionally terrifying and often uncomfortable, has also been positive. As always, the best absolutes lurk behind clichés: you don't know what you've got until it's gone . . . or at least nearly gone. Long-range or long-term anxieties, ambitions and preoccupations are thrown into a new perspective by the prospect of death, which has sometimes loomed with implacable imminence, only to turn away at the last minute. Both my sight, and my life itself, are things that I am relishing in what could easily be their last stages. I have lost one eye completely and after a detached retina operation have now disappeared behind bottle-bottomed glasses that enable me to see with the remaining eye. I have learned – at times of great weakness and fragility – how terrifying it must be to be the fragile and weak pensioner struggling through crowds, trying to keep up, trying to catch the bus, cross the road and get on the tube train, when even a white stick cannot guarantee a wide berth.

So there are wisdoms, affinities and new perspectives, and there are losses. My libido has never recovered from the three months of morphine used to treat my shingles. I seem to have left a sexual youth behind, and, as a result of its excesses, to have entered an early sexual retirement. But at the same time I have been sustained throughout my illness by the love of my partner, which has only underlined to me that sex and love live in similar worlds but are not locked together like the horse and cart of traditional love and marriage. There are battles to be fought on the immediate horizon, and AIDS has given me platforms that I might never otherwise have attained, but it has also given me issues and causes I never sought or expected to fight. It is perhaps the inevitable, but certainly the fabulous irony, that the threat of death has led to a heightened sense of life, for me personally, and for the gay community in general.

Michael Ignatieff

There's No Place Like Home: The Politics of Belonging

Certain social anxieties are an inseparable part of the very experience of being modern. One of these concerns the possibility of belonging. Is it possible to feel a sense of belonging to societies which change as rapidly as modern ones do, which are as explicitly divided – by race, class, gender and region – as modern ones are, and which are as driven by the power of money as capitalist modernity has been? The way the question is put suggests the answer. Modernity and belonging just don't go together: the incompatibility isn't simply a matter of the brutal temporariness of the modern social order. It's also a question of how the modern individual is put together, whether the modern self *wants* to belong in the ways that were available in the face-to-face intimacies of tribal and village life. Modernity's core value is freedom, especially the freedom to fashion one's identity and one's life as one will. Since our very sense of dignity and self-worth are tied into this idea of personal freedom, we tend to rank feelings of belonging – to community, nation, family – much lower than our ancestors in pre-industrial, pre-modern societies.

Yet when we rank our values in this way, we continue to hanker after the certainties and securities which our very choices have the effect of foreclosing. We may not believe that belonging is possible, but that hardly stops us wanting it. Belonging is not just a feeling of membership in a particular community – be it neighbourhood or nation – it is also a particular sense of understanding and being understood: understanding the wider world of social relations in which we live and feeling that those around us understand not merely what we say, but what we mean. Feeling at home, in other words, is a particular kind of cognitive as well as emotional experience. It is the sense that we can give a mental shape to the social world, and that, in this social world, what we do and say is comprehended by those around us.

Once this idea of understanding is put into the picture, we can begin to understand why belonging is so impermanent and so ironic a feeling in modern society. For modern social orders are radically complex places: the division of labour in which we earn our living and the market-place in which we buy and sell our goods are vast global organisms which are poorly understood, even by experts. The technologies we manipulate every day also escape the understanding of most of us, though we use them happily enough. Our picture of society is given to us largely by the media and we suspect, quite rightly, that neither they nor we have any very firm idea of what is actually going on. This does not mean that understanding modernity is impossible, merely that it is difficult, and that our social knowledge is made up of social myths and historical fantasies encrusted around a very small stock of private experiences whose testimony we trust simply because it is ours and we have often learned its truth the hard way.

The twin longings to understand the modern world and to master the forces which seem to have us in our grip are the impulses which drive modern politics. In this sense, all modern politics is about belonging, about creating the understandings and the institutional frameworks which enable us to believe that we do actually belong to communities called 'society' or 'nation' which in turn give us a collective means of exercising control over our private destinies. If the very legitimacy of politics is in question, at the end of the 1990s, it is because we do not seem able to devise policies to prevent the apparently unstoppable erosion of community, cohesion and the sense of civic belonging that seem the necessary accompaniment of late modernity.

Our nostalgia for civility, order and community is so deep that we have trouble facing the issue we began with, i.e. whether belonging is possible at all in modern societies like our own. The question is not whether we can make our societies more just and more fair; whether we can make them more efficient; whether we can, in sum, govern them in the interests of the majority. Fatalism about the possibilities of political action is uncalled for: the twentieth century offers several examples, the New Deal being the most benign, where societies which had almost despaired of political action managed, by dint of progressive reform, to restore public faith in the possibility of politics itself. So the question is not: can we make our societies fairer or most just? It is whether the pursuit of justice, fairness and efficiency can also deliver belonging, cohesion and community. On this question I believe, we should be sceptical.

Britain was the first state to attempt to reconcile a liberal social order with modern capitalism. Now it is struggling to find a politics capable of holding together the social order itself in the hurricane unleashed by the computer-driven economic revolution. The British debate is important because it has not been parochial. Its impact has been felt around the world, wherever the modern crisis of belonging is addressed.

When Mrs Thatcher famously remarked, in the mid 1980s, that there was 'no such thing as society', she sent a surge of delighted self-recognition through one section of the country and a shiver of anxiety through the other. The remark focused an entire country's concerns about its social cohesion. Her supporters felt she was taking aim at socialists' chief ideological totem – 'society' used as a moral abstraction to justify state interference. To her enemies, she was finally laying bare the inevitable results of her regime: the creation of a moral and social jungle. Since even some of her Conservative supporters squirmed at the bleak individualism of her vision, she was quick to evoke – and associate herself with – the emotions of national pride. There might be no such thing as society, she went on to say, but there was a nation, and such feelings of collective belonging as could be reconciled with free market competition could be safely directed to the nation's chief institutions – Parliament and the monarchy, and the traditions of political stability and civility conjured up by those magic words. The more anomic her vision of 'society', in other words, the more important it became for her to emphasise the stabilising virtues of patriotism or national belonging.

Now it is true that no politician since the war proved more effective in mobilising political support from the two nations, rich and poor, north and south, included and excluded. Her appeal across the class divide succeeded precisely because she understood that inequality in the

1970s had drained one-nation Toryism of its remaining credibility. Sociological cynicism was central to her success. She told the British people what they believed to be true, i.e. that class divisions were and are incorrigible. Collectivist social engineering was bound to fail and appeals to social cohesion, in a divided society, were nothing less than hypocritical. The only way for the crabs to crawl their way out of the barrel was to pile on top of each other; those with the sharpest claws and fiercest attack would crawl over the rim. Her appeal to individualism was plausible, paradoxically, because it seemed to understand the depths of class envy and antagonism so much better than those who preached harmony and consensus.

Likewise, in her appeal to British nationalism, she exploited native British chauvinism but was not a captive to it. She was, in her belligerent way, a more committed European than most of her electorate, as her robustly interventionist stance on Bosnia proves. The core of her objection to Europe was that the harmonisation of European social protection and employment law accompanying gradual federation would endanger British identity by reducing those divisions which are uniquely British. The social chapter would reduce Britain's competitive advantage as a low-wage, low-cost economy. A low-wage economy is, of necessity, an unequal one. She accepted with pride the sneer of other nations that Britain's class divisions make her what she is. It is just such divisions – experienced from childhood in her father's grocery – which engendered those driving passions of resentment, shame, envy and ambition that are alchemised by individuals into compensatory competition.

Her defence of inequality was electorally successful because she combined it with a spirited attack on the social archaism of the 'one nation' appeal. She mobilised all those who felt either humiliated by its paternalism or angry at its hypocrisy. Compared to the emollient tones of social resignation perfected by Harold Macmillan, her naked embrace of the hard realities of social division sounded both honest and bracing. She stood for a modern class system ordered exclusively by wealth and achievement rather than birth and inheritance: a porous elite open to the talents of bright, ambitious grocers' daughters. But the meritocratic accent did not conceal her underlying sociological relish towards the prospect of permanent – if always re-forming – class division.

Mrs Thatcher's sociological vision is, alas, not history. She remains the Delphic oracle of modern conservatism, not only in Britain but around the world. The meanings she attaches to 'society' and 'nation' – and the policies which have flowed from these meanings – continue to shape British society long after her political demise. Reaganism was an interlude compared to this, in part because the British parliamentary system delivers to a prime minister bent on ideological and economic reconstruction a degree of power which the American constitution explicitly forbids to the president. The sheer scale of her impact, incidentally, ought to have put paid to a cherished British image of itself as a nation safe from continental-style political enthusiasm, a country secure in its traditions and its continuities. This insular fable was not even true before Mrs Thatcher came to power. The scientific and industrial revolutions began here; as did the competitive market individualism which appalled European conservatives throughout the nineteenth century. The cliché of Britain as an island of political and social stability in a world of change was always false, but as long as the empire survived, it offered the refuge of convenient illusion. Since 1945, the illusion has been maintained, by left and right alike, but the imagery has soured: stability has come to seem like stasis, continuity like institutional paralysis. Whether framed in complacent or anxious terms, British exceptionalism is confirmed. In reality, Britain's post-1945 history was not exceptional. Like France, she had to shed an empire and modernise an outdated industrial and social structure. Like the rest of Europe, she had to adapt her geopolitical role in the light of the irresistible rise of American power. And, since 1945, she has managed to accomplish all these tasks without the success that conservatives usually claim, but also without the failures insisted upon by the left. Both the rhetoric of self-congratulation and the self-flagellation have missed out how much Britain has changed since the war. Far from being becalmed or stable, Britain has undergone three periods of revolutionary change in fifty years. The Attlee government created the post-war society of entitlement, the sixties created a new sexual, moral and aesthetic culture, and the Thatcher revolution sought to undo the first two and create a society of achievement. Two revolutions and a counter-revolution, then. In reality, they were three failed modernisations. The Attlee revolution began the retreat from empire and laid the basis for the welfare state but failed to address, or even fully see, the emerging crisis in British economic performance; the sixties revolution created the modern culture of self-expression and self-fulfilment but did nothing to reform an increasingly inefficient corporatist economy. The Thatcher revolution took up where these failed revolutions had left off: facing up to relative economic decline and facing down the so-called permissiveness of the preceding age. If there is widespread anxiety about social cohesion in Britain, it is because, first of all, there has been so much change since 1945, and so much of it seemed to consume the society's own image of itself as a stable, unchanging place.

In the 1990s we are in the midst of a reckoning on the record of this third and most convulsive of modernisations. The reckoning will probably be a damning one. The Labour Party is betting, with some plausibility, that millions of voters will recognise the truth in this picture of their society:

> Above all, we live in a new world of us and them. The sense of belonging to a successful national project has all but disappeared. Average living standards may have risen but have not generated a sense of well-being; if anything, there is more discontent because the gains have been spread so unevenly and are felt to be so evanescent. The country is increasingly divided against itself, with an arrogant officer class apparently indifferent to the other ranks it commands.
> (Will Hutton, *The State We're In*, 1995, p. 62)

Millions of voters agree with this diagnosis written by Will Hutton, the editor of the *Observer*, in a comprehensive survey of Britain's economic, social and political malaise.

The price of three failed modernisations has been high: increased inequality, decreased civility and a pervasive cynicism about the effectiveness of politics. The remedies proposed by New Labour are attractive: a 'stakeholding society' which combines republican reform of the constitution to renew political citizenship with reform of the economy and the welfare state to renew the sense of belonging to a national project. The aim, be it noted, is not simply improved economic performance, but increased social cohesion, neighbourliness, civic-mindedness and public activism. The attractive feature of proposals for a 'stake-holding society' is that it purports to address the perceived amorality of a society purely devoted to self-interest. The concept of a social 'stake' implies a desire to renew each individual's contractual commitment to society: rights confer responsibilities and state entitlements imply an obligation to be civil, law-abiding and neighbourly.

Yet it is worth looking closely at the expectations which Labour and its best thinkers are setting themselves, for they are dauntingly difficult to satisfy: not merely higher living standards, but a 'sense of well-being' and a sense of 'belonging to a successful national project'. Belonging and a sense of well-being are more easily conjured as rhetorical abstractions than made real by legislation and collective action. There is certainly a real anxiety in Britain that 'we' no longer know who 'we' are; that we do not know what 'we' owe each other; that we do not know what we 'belong' to. The very words 'society' and 'nation' slide between irony and piety, losing content and focus as we use them. Undoubtedly it would be good if more of us felt we belonged to a 'successful national project'. Yet it is hard to imagine how to give practical substance to such metaphysical aspirations.

It is difficult enough, as fifty years of recent British politics should attest, to raise average living standards. Raising the average sense of well-being, whatever that means, would be more difficult still. In fact, as environmentalists never cease to tell us, raising average living standards might actually reduce an average sense of well-being. Every additional car may increase the living standard of the individual who purchases it but decrease the general well-being of those obliged to endure clogged roads and fouled air. Rising living standards and well-being are ambiguously related at the best of times, and not simply for ecological reasons. In principle, well-being is a contestable good. Your idea of well-being may not be mine. In particular, it isn't clear how a sense of well-being and a sense of belonging are connected. Or rather, we can make the direct connection only by privileging one kind of well-being over all others, i.e. the one which comes with a strong sense of civic and patriotic attachment. Needless to say, Will Hutton's powerful and passionate polemic makes just such an assumption: that all right-thinking people will wish to participate actively in the affairs of their country. This is a flattering assumption, but it finesses a difficulty about liberty. If it's only order, cohesion and civility that you want, you'd be happy in Lee Kuan Yew's Singapore. A civic society should also be a free one. Individuals ought to be free in their patriotism. They should choose their belonging, their level and degree of civic attachment. From which it follows that many will choose precious little attachment at all. Many indeed will choose to remain 'free riders', benefiting from services and entitlements to which they contribute little, if anything. A free society is bound to be a wasteful one, sustained by the activism of a minority rather than the active involvement of a majority.

Even the active minority will feel torn between conflicting claims and loyalties. Citizenship, however valuable, is only one of our identities. We belong to families, work-groups, networks of friends, private and public associations of all kinds. These forms and sites of belonging present us with constant conflicts of loyalty: how much time, how much effort, how much money can we afford to devote to each of these spheres. The privatisation of modern life is much lamented – families enclosed upon themselves, drawing up the drawbridge around their lives to the exclusion of their neighbours, connected to the wider society only through the distorting mirror of television and radio. But privacy is also a good thing, and if modern life is more private and less civic, this, at least in part, reflects ordinary people's real preferences.

Not all privatisation, however, is freely chosen. To the degree that this privatisation has been forced on people, a politics of belonging can and should do something to reverse the trend. Good public services and safe streets strengthen family life while drawing families out of the 'fortress home' into a shared public sphere. Here, the strengthening of family values and citizenship go hand in hand. But in other cases, citizenship and family life may not be as easily reconciled. The modern suburban family has a relentless appetite for housing, supermarkets and highways. The attempt to strengthen suburban family life by providing these goods puts other civic goods – such as green site land – under increasing strain.

The problem is not merely that citizenship and privacy are often in conflict. What nuclear families want from the public sphere and what those living outside nuclear families want are difficult to reconcile. A policy for renewing citizenship by 'strengthening' the family is certain to discriminate, in some way or other, against the rising numbers of people who are childless, or live alone or whose family arrangements do not conform to the nuclear norm. This splintering of society, into groups whose interests and attitudes are necessarily in conflict, is *wrongly understood* if it is seen negatively as fragmentation or disintegration. In most cases, it is powered by a desire to live a life expressive of one's own needs and choices.

As these opportunities for significant life-choice multiply, so does the conflict, in principle, between freedom and belonging. We all sense this conflict daily, between wanting to get involved and wanting to be left alone, between wanting to share responsibility for some task or duty, and between wanting to slough it off on others, between attending to our own needs and those of our families and between attending to those of the strangers with whom we share our society. These conflicts are the very essence of being the social animals we are. They can never be conjured away by any social engineering we can imagine. Our anxieties about what we owe society and what society owes us, our dilemmas about how to resolve these claims, are integral to the very idea of belonging itself. To belong is to have the right to choose. It is a conflictual, rather than an easeful state, and the sense of well-being it imparts is rather ambiguous. If you're looking for well-being, you might get more reliable results if you choose a life of radical selfishness. While it is delusive to suppose that private affluence can be meaningfully appreciated in an environment of public squalor, it is also pious to suppose that private well-being necessarily requires any very extensive degree of participation in public decision-making.

It is also a delusion to suppose that belonging in a modern democracy can ever imply sharing in a political consensus. Yet this is what phrases like 'a sense of belonging to a successful national project' implies. In reality, the portion of the country which votes for a Labour administration will roughly share its view of what percentage of the national income should be spent renewing the social infrastructure, and the percentage that didn't will bitterly resent the tax increases which will result. Broad social agreement is possible only if the policies generate sufficient economic growth to meet as many competing claims as possible. In this sense alone could it be said that Germans, for example, felt a sense of belonging to a successful national project. Yet even fifty years of extraordinary economic success have not stilled the profound and sometimes violent conflict within

German society about its relation to the past, the nature of its commitment to democracy and, above all, the morally ambivalent nature of its economic success. In these circumstances, which are natural not merely to Britain, but to any mature political society, it would be more fruitful to think of a sense of belonging residing, not in the loose idea of social consensus, as in a sense of inclusion in what is certain to be a sharply polarised debate about objectives and priorities.

The aspiration for social cohesion and consensus is the unstated aim of much of the republican agenda in New Labour. The proposals for a new Bill of Rights, abolition of the vote of the hereditary peerage, modernisation of the monarchy, are not institutional house-cleaning or modernisation for modernisation's sake. They are intended to address the widely felt disaggregation and incoherence of Britain's elements of national identity. Creeping republicanism is intended to give us a modern British state that we can all admire. The intention of constitutional reformers is to displace the sullenly resentful and chauvinistic ethnic nationalism of the white British bulldog with a modern civic nationalism built around attachment to institutions which respect the rights of citizens and which conceive of the nation as a community of equals, not as a pyramid of subjects. Again, these are desirable objectives but, even if attained, they are unlikely to still the disquiet and debate about British national identity. The republican agenda seeks to render one vision of our identity hegemonic, but the other – monarchical, deferential, traditional, rooted in a history of empire abroad and class division at home – still calls forth devoted loyalty. It is condescending to suppose it will slip away without a whimper, and politically naive to suppose that constitutional reform itself will create a new national consensus. National identity everywhere, and not just in Britain, is a site of conflicted meanings, and only our nostalgia for a fictive past leads us to imagine an end to the conflict. What brings tears to the eyes of some generations will be a joke to later ones; a symbol which rouses one ethnic group to fury will give pride and comfort to another. A republican reform of the constitution may modernise the state, but this will not and cannot still the interminable, and properly conflictual, debate about what it means to be British, and what, if anything, we have reason to be proud about.

Men and women, black and white, young and old, immigrant and long-time resident are simply bound to disagree about our national identity. This plurality of values is not a misunderstanding or a mistake. It is inherent in the ways in which individuals take their values from the groups they belong to. It does not follow that a society of value pluralism is necessarily a violent society. All our anxieties about the cohesion of a multi-racial, multi-ethnic society crystallise around the image of progressively deepening incomprehension, social separatism and antagonism which supposedly follows. Yet this underestimates the interest all groups have in playing by the minimal rules of the game – the rule of law and the practice of tolerance. Competing groups who disrespect each other's values may tolerate each other and co-exist simply because the advantages of common adherence to the rules outweigh the benefits of social warfare. Provided – and it is a big if – the liberal state consistently guarantees procedural fairness to all groups, there is no reason in principle why they cannot compete and disagree peacefully. Anxieties about the cohesion of multi-racial societies are in fact not about cohesion, but about difference, about accepting otherness. If we can accept otherness, we can at least secure the minimum belonging afforded by a common life under the regime of procedural fairness.

The agenda of constitutional reforms, first publicised by organisations like Charter 88 and incorporated into New Labour's election programme – electoral Upper House, elected mayors, Bill of Rights, regional assemblies – will certainly improve the procedural fairness and accountability of the British state. These ends alone make them worthy of support. Whether they will make ordinary citizens feel they belong, whether they will enhance civic participation and foster civic activism are much more difficult questions to answer. Much is made of the attractions of feeling oneself to be a citizen rather than a subject. A creeping republicanisation of British institutions is proposed, not simply to modernise an archaic state but to give people a sense that the state is theirs and must be responsive to their demands and needs. Institutional reform is perceived not simply as an end in itself but as a means towards ambitious spiritual objectives. Turning us all into citizens is supposed to re-forge the civic bond and deepen our attachment to each other, to society and nation. It is questionable whether worthy but prosaic constitutional re-plumbing can accomplish such prodigies of moral regeneration. Those who most strongly support constitutional reform do so because they want the feeling of belonging to a modern, rather than an archaic, state, a state which explicitly respects their rights and acknowledges their entitlements. How far this desire for civic belonging spreads through the population is hard to determine, and how to satisfy this desire in day-to-day life is not obvious.

Our anxieties about living in a social jungle, about the disintegration of social cohesion and civility are not addressed adequately by proposals for constitutional reform. Too much spiritual good is expected to come out of a change in the law. In any event, the middle classes are much less in need of enfranchising civic reform than the poor and excluded. The real test of reform is whether it can do something about the practical experience of visiting a police station, a benefit office or a public hospital. These are rarely experiences which leave any of us with a revivified sense of citizenship, and yet what else is citizenship than the belief that public authorities have an obligation to treat us with respect as citizens? Translating such moral objectives into practical politics is more than a matter of constitution-making. It means attacking the embedded culture of cruelty and condescension in which benefit claimants, particularly, have to live most of their encounters with the state.

Nor will equality be enough. Treating everyone as equal often ends up by treating each individual as a number. The ideology of equality, even when translated into good institutional practice, may result only in impersonality. If people are going to feel they have a stake in society, they want the inequality of their stakes acknowledged; they want their individuality as persons to be recognised; they want their special needs met. There is thus a conflict between equality and belonging, and its resolution is not evident. It is an open question, as I wrote more than a decade ago in *The Needs of Strangers*, 'whether any welfare system can reconcile this contradiction between treating individuals equally and treating each individual with respect.' M. Ignatieff, *The Needs of Strangers*, (1984, p.17)

Nor will 'a defence of the welfare state' in itself deliver us a practical politics of belonging. After the Thatcher revolution, nostalgia for the lost stabilities and decencies of the welfare state is understandable. In the presence of beggars, homeless people and bedless mental patients at the gates of our underground stations, it is natural to wish oneself back to a time when the welfare state supposedly 'coped' with these problems and, in coping, afforded those of us in employment the illusion that we lived in a decent society.

Yet the solidarities created by the welfare state have a degree of moral ambiguity over which our nostalgia for vanished decencies draws a convenient veil. While the provision of common services - swimming-baths, leisure centres, public transport – did create a public sphere which brought the classes together in shared moments of common life, the welfare state also kept rich and poor apart. The intention, of course, was to end the indignities and condescensions that went hand in hand with charitable and philanthropic relations between rich and poor. But in ending these face-to-face relations – and often the moral torment that accompanied them – the welfare state encouraged a moral division of labour in which the misfortunes and life calamities of others were kept hidden from the fortunate by armies of social workers, benefit administrators and local government officers. So that now, when middle class people cite the beggars and homeless adolescents on our streets as a sign of social dissolution, their moral disquiet has an element of ambiguity: are they merely wishing to have such disturbing scenes safely tucked out of sight? The welfare state may not have created the reality of social cohesion as much as its illusion, by sweeping the poor and the disturbed into an archipelago of state services.

The impact of the welfare state on the discharge of private family obligation has also been ambiguous. When, for example, social workers take over the caring functions formerly discharged by family members, there is both a gain and a loss; dependent individuals may receive better care in public institutions and family members – women, especially – will be freed to enter the labour market or to use their time in other ways. But it also true that a sense of family obligation may suffer, as anyone can see from the numbers of unvisited elderly relatives in public care. More generally, community ties among strangers may be weakened when everyone comes to believe it is the 'council's job'. The paradoxical effect of a welfare-state culture in which everyone assumes that the elderly, the ill and the incapable are visited by some social worker or other is that neighbours cease to think of it as their duty too to look after those who are lonely and alone. The welfare state has not always increased social cohesion and mutual responsibility: it has also fostered patterns of social isolation and disengagement. 'It's the council's job' has entered the vocabulary as a new style of moral disengagement.

The middle classes have proved the most assiduous beneficiaries of the welfare state, in particular using state-funded education to improve their life chances and those of their children. Hence the welfare state contained but did not reduce social inequality. Its existence afforded the middle class the agreeable sensation that they lived in a moral community. But whether poor claimants in benefit offices, dying indigents in state hospitals or the long-term unemployed felt a similar sense of social solidarity is doubtful. Post-war social assistance was certainly less stigmatising than the dole and the poor-house, but it has never eradicated the sense of shame associated with state dependency. This is a surprising result, given the extent to which welfare was re-defined, in the post-war settlement, as a right. The benefit a claimant receives by right ought not, in theory, to be a matter of shame or resentment. In practice, the entrenchment of rights and entitlements has not eradicated the culture of shame attached to welfare dependency. Neither has it eradicated the resentment of the contributors. It is fanciful to expect that even improved funding of the welfare state will cause these sensations of social division and mutual alienation to disappear. Britain's moderate economic success after the war appeared to make it possible to fund social solidarity without too much strain. As long as the middle classes could count on stable employment for themselves and their children and a modestly rising standard of living, the social contract implied by the welfare state seemed well worth paying, especially as they benefited themselves from access to its services. The casualisation of middle-class service employment, with the resultant loss of job security, has re-opened all the class resentment at the economic costs of social solidarity. Because the wealthier parts of the middle class diverted their rising real incomes into private education, pensions and health care – and now are stuck with the costs – they particularly resent paying taxes for a system they no longer use.

It would be self-evidently better if the welfare state were better funded: if state pensions were increased so that the middle class need not engage in the alienating and futile attempt to opt out; if, likewise, public education could be improved so that all classes receive something like a decent start in life; if public transport, parks, swimming-baths and leisure centres could be funded so that a common, and commonly respected, public sphere could be maintained. All of this would make for a society which is more efficient, more fair and more just. Nothing in what has been argued should be taken to imply that these are not desirable or practicable political goals. What is in question is the effect of such measures on feelings of social belonging and on measures of social cohesion. The impact on levels of crime, for example, is entirely unpredictable. Even harder to predict would be the impact on feelings of the civility of the culture.

Our anxieties about belonging, it seems to me, are a function of expectations which we cannot hope to meet.

To put the matter differently, we are nostalgic for a belonging we never had and risk a politics of endless frustration if we pursue a goal never previously achieved. We need to distinguish between justice and fairness – which are attainable in different degrees, and belonging – which does not necessarily follow from either.

Any discussion of our millennial anxieties about social cohesion and social belonging must begin and end with Mrs Thatcher, and not simply because her regime had such damaging effects on both. The real challenge, both of her views and of her policies, is that her acceptance of the necessity of social competition between classes might just be more sociologically realistic than those who put the political priority on social cohesion and social co-operation. It is a measure of her impact on the political consciousness of her country that the only remaining 'one nation Tories' left in Britain are Tony Blair's New Labour. It is now the British left – if it can be described as such – which seeks to restore civility, decency, cohesion and a sense of belonging to British life. These are admirable goals, and they may be politically appealing, but there is no disguising their deeply conservative (with a small c) character. It is not that an appeal to justice and fairness has dropped out of the moral register: it is that these goals are held to be desirable to the degree that they promote social unity. This makes them subservient to a moral objective which may be unattainable. There is no right answer, in principle, to the question of how to reconcile the conflict we feel, as individuals and as a society, between the claims of freedom and the claims of belonging. Each of us will answer this question differently, and any politics worth supporting ought to respect our right to frame our own lives by the answers we give. The belonging that modernity makes possible is bound to be local, particular and transient: to this person, to that family, to this neighbourhood or that place for a particular period of our lives. But this does not exclude bigger commitments. To the degree that our society and our politics provide us with the larger frame in which these contingent and local belongings are secured, we can muster a larger loyalty to society and nation. The loyalty will never be whole-hearted, the belonging never unmingled with alienation. But only those who dream of an undivided heart and a reconciled mind will wish it otherwise.

Michael Neve

Nuclear Fallout: Anxiety and the Family

Familial anxiety: what is the true story? At first sight the answer seems clear: it is the story of the possible death of safety. No safe harbours, no parents, no direction home. The family is the place of peace as well as safety and it is being threatened. That is anxiety.

But the range and diversity of the anxiety itself needs attention. Is the situation so much out of control, so eerie, that the family is itself being misunderstood, being taken as a safe house when it cannot be one, being taken as an answer when it is part of the question? Maybe it would be helpful to discuss a proposal that at first sight seems scary and irrational – that the family is not the real focus of the anxiety. Let the anxiety out, out of the house and into the world and what does it discover, about the world and about the interior of family life itself?

Put it another way. There are real anxieties, about real social dangers and varieties of collapse, and some of these involve people – adolescents or younger – still living at home. But in what sense is the *family* either the cause of, or the guard against, these dangers? The statistics on divorce and single mothers are there sure enough (299,197 marriages in 1993 and 165,018 divorces; 215,536 births outside marriage out of a total of 664,726 births), and only a fool would propose that these social facts are merely political products, products of Thatcherism, say, and not partly independent of them. But what is the politics of *then* proposing that the family is the solution, a site of restoration and that those who disagree are culpable?

Anxiety and its expression almost always involves exaggeration. Personal fears easily turn on a heightened sense of danger – it only takes one friend to be mugged and a whole city can become a dark and nasty place. No amount of statistical information to the contrary dislodges the fear. But the amplification of anxiety may also be a policy, a device, used by interested parties to instil an exaggerated fear for certain ends. In discussing the Ripper murders of 1888 in her book, *City of Dreadful Delight*, the historian Judith Walkowitz examined the various ways that the murders were reported to place them not in an actual world, but in a world of melodrama, of fear, of disputed ways that male and female sexual independence was being contested. Media coverage and response varied and even ideas of 'investigation' were saturated in larger disputes over conventional male preserves, the 'new woman' and the nature of sexual danger. Whether late Victorian London could be a terrain where women could be independent, happy and outside – these were the issues that emerged in the 'reporting' of the Ripper murders, and anxiety was amplified to promote a larger cause. A covert policing of social roles was part of the reporting purpose, which then received a feminist response. Anxiety was manufactured and then rebutted, while the war of images carried on.

I would argue that something of the same thing is happening in current debates about the family. We have the epic stories of the holy family torn asunder (the royal family) and the apparently united family devouring its own children (the Wests). And yet there is no real public discussion as to what might be the implications of these two sagas as regards the health of the family. Why cannot our generation join a vast historical chorus of voices that expresses unease with certain family arrangements and make our own new version of family?

The family has been an object of serious attention from historians for many years and offers various lessons for an age anxious about family fortunes. The first is quite simply that the history of the family is a history of change and variation, not just in size and organisation but in attitudes towards work, discipline and roles. The second and important point is that there is very little real evidence that the history of caring for and about family members developed with the nuclear family of the modern era. It isn't as though the family is something that displays a history of improved feeling, of increasing humanity. Historians being historians, there has been much argument over all this: (historians have their own history of consistent feeling, and it's called bile!). But the hard evidence is that the death of children, say, was as much a pain and a distress in 1600 as in 1900 when life expectation and family size were quite noticeably different from the present. The likely death of infants meant you had to have a tougher heart, but a heart none the less. It's clearly true that attitudes toward divorce have changed strikingly over time and it's also true that the property settlements for divorced women have changed enormously. But to suppose the nuclear family to be either separable from economic forces or to be the repository of advanced and humane feelings is mistaken. It is as much a historical creation as anything else, made possible by the growth of a commercial economy and of wealth. It is true that attitudes to, say, corporal punishment vary as that history unfolds, and that a certain eighteenth-century stress on sentiment coincides with the origins of the modern family. The historical work on the family by writers like Lawrence Stone, Peter Laslett and Linda Pollock has not settled the argument and Stone in particular holds that the nuclear family did bring a change in attitudes towards childhood and family virtues. But, taken as a whole, there is little evidence that the fate of family members was a matter of *indifference* in the pre-modern family. Indeed one of the problems with the school of thought propounding Victorian values is that some of those values seem harsher and more class-based than the Enlightenment values that preceded them. The Victorian nuclear family may, paradoxically, be a bad historical example of the values that the phrase itself is meant to evoke.

The history lesson, children, is that there is no such thing as an Ideal Family, no Platonic Playground. Furthermore, the complaints and the irritations have always been there. You get political radicals in the seventeenth century pining for patriarchy, you get eighteenth-century folk hostile to arranged marriage and (roughly) pro-love and pro-sentiment and you then get the Victorians chastising the eighteenth-century marriage for its being too liberal and too unchristian. And then you get a variety of Lytton Stracheys mocking the Victorians. It is entirely consistent with the history of the family that we now have our own critique and our own ideas for a different future. The place of monogamy is no longer guaranteed or thought to represent health or civilisation.

The implications for marriage and the family of biotechnology, sperm banks, artificial insemination and changes in the sexual division of labour are huge and hugely underdiscussed. But the vital point is that the history of confusion, fears about what may be lost, and what needs to be done are as old as the varieties of family. There is no historical watchtower that gives permanent views of a shifting landscape.

Current anxiety about the demise of the nuclear family *per se*, and the possibility that we are heading *towards* the cruel past, the past of child poverty, childhood disturbance and permanent economic emergency, is entirely to be expected. No one can honestly argue that changes in family structure will be easy or pleasant. The future does look difficult and there are people who are going to get hurt. What is not at all clear is whether the nuclear family is something to which we should be aspiring. And it's almost a scandal that it is the Victorian family, which generated a literature screaming with misery or loneliness or cruelty, that has been confected as a family romance with all that volume turned off, except for a soundtrack combining muzak and moral niceties in equal measure.

The first context that has to be established is the confined historical time and place of the 'happy family' and the near certainty of its disappearance. Before all the talk about divorce and sixties irresponsibility and the rounding up of the usual suspects, it has to be remembered that the nuclear family is a very brief visitor at the social history table and that family structure has economic roots that are crucial and which put fierce talk about moral questions on the sidelines. And getting this wrong and insisting on fantasies of family life is by no means confined to one particular political party or ideology. From the right we have the John Redwoods, scourge of single parents and punishing transgression against the nuclear family by the threat of withdrawing benefits. From the left, New Labour emerges though its Mandelson spin doctor with largely the same agenda, but using the carrot rather than the stick, with its picture of a generation of happy young couples glued together by the notion of a public dowry.

In both cases it is a particular kind of family that is being praised or disparaged and the distressing thing about modern Britain is that so little time is given to the history lesson and so much to the cynical use of nostalgia. Cynical, because the family ideal is invoked at the very time when the economic realities have broken the ideal itself.

Long-term unemployment, the need for two incomes per family, no tax-breaks for child care and the refusal to endorse European guidelines for paternity leave.

Come on, let's admit it: Thatcherism undermined economically what it endorsed ideologically. Of course it would be misleading to propose that Thatcherism was entirely responsible for economic distress: the forces behind economic change are in some cases international and outside political control. But the conservative moral call is for structures and behaviours that are too inflexible and historically too local and particular for the tasks the future will bring. The fault in Thatcherite politics is not to admit its own historical limitations and to go on subsidising the chorus of ideological sounds that it insists are timeless, are eternal verities. (Mrs Thatcher may not have thought there was any such thing as society, but she certainly believed that there were individuals and families.) This moral revivalism will none the less keep playing, unless someone can reach in and turn it off. The chorus is repetitive, it covers a multitude of sins, but there is a vast investment in keeping it on because the alternative would be to go back to history and politics and end the moral interrogation.

The economic confusions sit uneasily with the other big question: the casual connection between the breakdown in family forms and crime. The argument for the prosecution goes something like this. That the family should/could be the home of moral sense and moral education and is failing to be so. And the reason for this failure falls largely on to the shoulders of a group that conservatives have long described as sixties liberals. As a now familiar set of journalists, radio discussants and politicians proclaim, has not sixties selfishness and confusion undermined the family as the cornerstone, the birthplace even, of a morally imaginative community? And in a country where the state is withdrawing from full state security from cradle to grave, thus putting even more pressure on the family unit to provide stability and a sense of belonging, won't this deliberate subversion lead inevitably to chaos – both economic and moral?

In fact the withdrawal of the granny state is itself a contradiction, in that the state does indeed begin an economic withdrawal and calls up its private sector to replace it, while doing so in the most grannyish kind of way. There is no family silver, but there is an extremely noisy granny at the end of the empty table telling us why that is a good thing and making sure we have no way of interrupting. Thus we also have to remain silent as the lecture proceeds to the naming of absent friends who have not listened properly and are being punished elsewhere – the single mother, the divorced couple, the absent father. Yet my own experience and conviction tells me that some of the most imaginative and secure alternatives to the nuclear family are the work of precisely the people named as culprits by current writers, and that the attack on them (in the name of morality and anxiety) needs to be fought. What is my experience? I have three children by two mothers, to one of whom I was married but am no longer. The children spend as much time as possible with each other and me and all know the story. By historical standards, this is a very mild contribution to the annals of human turpitude but is now almost enough to make one an enemy of the state. Let's be honest – my children certainly experienced distress at separation and know that many of their friends have different lives, lives that may be more like the norm. But the important point is that they haven't automatically been damaged by it, as some commentators would have us believe. They have felt and thought and talked about it. And they still have their own lives: they have rows with their own friends; they go on and off people and they work these things out. Likewise, they don't appear incapable of understanding why adults get divorced and the pain they go through. Indeed they don't like adults treating them as if they were not capable of being part of the solution and not part of the problem. They don't need to be treated like 'children' (I shall return to those inverted commas later) and they don't like being over-protected. They develop in ways that absorb distress, distress they didn't ask for, and only sentimentality suggests otherwise. They can feel loved and pissed off at the same time, and this 'ordinary unhappiness' can be managed. So how is it that all the reasons for being hopeful are never heard, in examples like mine, and all we get is a guarantee of nemesis? Why do we not even deem it likely that there are happy untraditional families? Why does it not get publicly proposed that these happy untraditional families could be the families of the future?

The idea of family values as an intrinsic good is obviously odd for those who have experienced family difficulties as children. I had such experiences, but I never thought of my respectable and conservative parents as guilty of a bad marriage, nor did I ever see their subsequent divorce as a hollow victory for hedonistic egoism and moral laxity. I saw agony and necessity coming to terms. It's also true that the literature of the day on the psychiatric traps within family life was much more radical than that touted now. Much of it was influenced by the Scottish psychiatrist R.D. Laing, who had turned against conventional psychiatry and against conventional ideas of the family. Laing in that sense takes his place as just one of the doubters on the intrinsic values of the family who fill the historical story depicted earlier.

Using ideas from existentialist writers and from his own clinical experience, Laing came to see the family as a bleak world of double binds, contradictions and silences: a breeding-ground of social pathology. Some of his writings were helpful, even though they now show a harsh, parent-blaming side that was less obvious at the time. My point is that the attempted burial of this literature and of Laing in particular is a loss, a loss that is orchestrated by the routinised anti-sixties rhetoric now dominant. Family life as a deeply disturbing one, one that needed exposure and maybe avoidance, is now off the agenda. Think of two expressions that seem most dated and you get 'Laingian' and 'redistributive taxation'. These are yesterday's cries, sure, but what is odd is how they have been completely jettisoned, without in the Laingian case any idea that there were insights to be gained and used. And kept. That a lot of the cultural production of the sixties was false or trivial still leaves a lot that has life and truth. And this is not what you hear, especially if the discussion is about the family. Even the possibility that what is being offered as a moral and social stronghold might, in some cases, be a hell on earth, a 'normal family' hell, is dismissed. The conservative mind at this point says that this is in fact an abnormal example. But if there had not been an anti-familial cry for help, endorsed by some trained observers, who would ever have known? And who will hear these cries in the future?

The frightening thing about the call for the family to restore values and to fight off the dangers of alleged social breakdown is that one simple point is repressed: that the family is not the means whereby the required task can be performed. It is often unstable, a world of challenges between parents and children and between couples, and this is often for very good reasons. Quite apart from families that clearly don't work at all (and conservatives and their opponents share an understanding as to those), the truth about the 'normal' family is that the development of its members requires challenge, requires risk, requires what is often seen by parents as betrayal. Betrayal because the child's development needs secrecy and eventually the overthrow of parental authority. If this dimension to the story is rubbed out in the name of Victorian sentimentality, then the family can indeed appear like a constant unit bathing in the light of respectability and timeless trust. But behind all those lace curtains, from Malmesbury to Montrose, what is actually being experienced? Laing saw certain things, and says in some recently published interviews that the normal family was for him a deadening, mundane, eventless world. Everybody fitted, nobody talked, and 'that sort of dead family is absolutely essential for the function of the type of society we still have.' That was Laing in 1987–8. Less fiercely, but still anxious about the family as unstable in both its normal and abnormal forms, let's try an update.

Anxious not about the family itself but about the need to be especially good parents, parents *à la* Spock, *à la* Penelope Leach, the modern couple turn the child into the household oracle, the endangered species whose needs and whose happiness are the fundamentals. In a world that is genuinely dangerous, the child is protected and then overprotected, sealed off by television or the motor car. That is the work of anxiety, all of it understandable. What then happens is that the risk-taking that underlies normal development becomes stylised and artificial. Modern teenagers have already had to learn a language of cool, of credibility, but in a sealed-off world. The child becomes the recipient of anxiety and the household oracle or tyrant. Or both. The child is accorded a premature capacity for certainty and a knowledge of what he or she really wants that are forms of adult fiction, fictions that adults write for children because the family has to be built on solid rock. Or, more alarmingly, the child is deployed in the fights between parents and is said to want *x* or *y*, is presented as a rational agent when in truth no consultation has taken place. It's that world that children least like, the one that either infantilises them or sees them (and uses them) as a cross between Judy Garland and Immanuel Kant.

Spending more time with your family is the theme tune of the modern age (an age when both parents may be working) and it speaks of acute anxiety. But it's not a good anxiety, this: it's inside when it should be outside, it's anxious about *children* when it should be anxious about their *world*, a world where adults can leave children alone. So children become prematurely knowing, seem to be less and less childish, while the adults become more and more childish and anxious. Out in the consumer world, the story peaks. Adults pretend to be frightened by *Jurassic Park*, because it would be wrong not to be. Adults take second place because, if they did not, they would be failing their children. Result? Everybody is infantilised. Everybody looks about nineteen years old, all of the time. But at least the family is intact.

What are the adults doing this for? They are forgetting their own needs, or at least appearing to, and as a result are beginning a new kind of family disturbance. Not least with that most anti-familial of human urges, sexual love. The commitment to the family, the sheer fatigue that it exacts, brings the marginalisation of adult need. Adult needs come to seem suspect. Opponents deliberately distort this by arguing that this is not true – look at divorce. That is a need being met, and at a high price. But divorce is not a *need*, except when needs are not being met. Certain ideas of family life make the chance of adults having room for their needs almost nil. We all know of marriages that did not work because there was not enough room for two people. We should also speak of families that are shaky and difficult because of expectations for children (expressed on their behalf by adults) leading to the early demise of adulthood. All this can be modified, but not when the nuclear happy family is asked to embody ideals and the training for ideals that it cannot and ought not to meet.

Those who want a nation of head prefects, stable family units, a minimum state support apparatus and who still hope for maturity and adulthood ought to ponder the real reasons for asking so much of the family. I often feel that the true aim is a nation of half-adults, voting Tory, without any adult opposition, surrounded by a sea of half-adult children whose cynical language is an index of inexperience and buried anxiety. It's almost as if the urgency of the family ideal matters more, its performance matters more, than love and what love can do. And it certainly matters more than what adults are meant to do when love has died. I personally believe that a liberal attitude to divorce – one hardly dares even say this – allows separated couples a real chance of getting on fairly well in that lovely

ESSENTIAL PAPERS

ON SUICIDE

EDT.

MALTSBERGER AND

GOLDBLATT

Café Internet

Category	Item	Price
Access	Standard (½ hour)	£3.00
	Concession	£2.50
	10 Session	£22.50
	10 Session Concession	£20.00
Print, Copy & Fax	B&W Print /Copy	20p
	B&W Concession	15p
	Colour Print / Copy	75p
	Concessions	50p
	UK Fax	£1, then 75p per extra page

		extra page
Email	Email Account	£1.00 p/w (min £5)
	Quarterly A/C	£12 incl. Disk
	Annual	£40 incl. Disk
Consumables	Floppy disk	£1.25
Consultancy / Training	Half Hour Hosted	£10 per person
	2 Hour Training	£25 per person
	General Consultancy	£40 per hour
	Bespoke Training	£ negotiable

Café Internet, 2nd Floor, Waterstone's Bookshop
153-157 Sauchiehall Street, Glasgow G2 3EW
0141 353 2484 glasgow@cafeinternet.co.uk

land we sixties rebels cherish so much: looking after children and ourselves after the parting. But this is England, and you aren't going to hear too much about the good conduct of divorced couples who put the child at the front after divorce.

The anti-authoritarian writings of the sixties, now so despised, at least glimpsed this, which brings us to a further point. Why is it not possible that *anti-authoritarian* writing and writers are in fact *authoritative*? Why assume that the sixties parent is undisciplined, hostile to education, morally lax and the perfect target for ideological onslaught? It is a very bad mistake, because one reason for being dubious about family experience is how little it contributes to the maintenance of the values that families are now said to embody.

It has to be admitted that the sixties generation has been very divided about the issues, and – on the family question in particular – has often failed to generate real alternatives. When push comes to shove, there are ten couples from that generation tolerating adultery and going through the moral motions for every one couple thinking out an alternative. In ways that would not have surprised the now almost unread Angus Wilson, the generation of rebels is turning out to be more conventional than that of its parents – less romantic, less humorous in its ideas of personal life, maybe even less courageous, given the economic circumstances. The anxiety generated here is in fact the sound of a generation 'rediscovering' conventional wisdom and wondering how to admit this in a suitably chastened way. Those who are divorced will know that there is nothing quite like getting a lecture about the mistaken nature of divorce from an ex-divorcee! Seeing at least some of the sixties generation turn into the skeletons in their own cupboards is not a pretty sight. It's one of the reasons for admiring - indeed needing – those who have not pretended that they were 'like that once but are now grown up'. But it's not impossible that one of the reasons the conservative family tape keeps running is that the message is falling on ears that were once alive to the alternative life but which have turned to the old story and approve it. The suddenly knowing and unforgiving grown-ups – we must learn to recognise them among our own (ex-)friends.

The making of strange alliances and the oversimplicity of assuming that an us-and-them model is sufficient is noticeably at work in the contemporary experience of fathers. At first sight, there is no real issue here. Fathers are absent, fathers are not paying up, fathers are guilty of domestic violence and sexual deception. The legal and informal attempts to rectify this are all for the good, since the alternative is abandonment and poverty. All true. But what about the other story, the story that even dares to introduce the father who has been equally - but no more – guilty, who has no intention of not paying up, who has lost the house and become the homesick non-custodial parent? Why is it so difficult, so like special pleading, to attempt to conjure this figure? Homesick fathers? Come on, that just means guilty fathers, fathers who regret what they have done and can't live with the consequences and are now going around lost and confused.

Nothing could be further from the truth. He is not homesick about marriage or indeed about 'home'. The place he misses is one where the contact with adults and children is not determined by the sentimental idea of the family. Indeed if that idea was not paramount, the homesick father might have a 'home' even after the failure of his marriage. Now, he probably thinks the office, his friend's couch or the cinema is his home. The homesick father (like the homesick mother) was probably homesick while married and is now living it out on the open road. Stop the fetishisation of the 'happy family', and the homesick fathers of this life might get a better hearing, without looking doomed and crazy in the world of Big Macs at the weekend or servile and silly when the ex-wife goes to the south of France for three weeks without the children. The homesick father knows that marriage and isolation are not home. His homesickness is a function of how few other people share that knowledge with him.

Personal experience has to play a part here, but other examples generate some of the following thoughts about the future of the family. One is another of life's little ironies: that the punitive policies of the Child Support Agency have usurped feminist initiatives and preyed on common fears, and the outcome is the homesick father. Now, please, I am entirely aware that there are absent fathers putting money into their new love's bank account to shield the scale of their wealth and to avoid paying their full whack. A lot of good they did the rest of us, who are now exposed to nasty state investigation on the ground that we deserve no less. But the truth is that measures like this are helping to produce a class of broken fathers. These two apparently opposed groups (feminists and opponents of the Lord Chancellor's divorce reforms) even use the same phrases: about not really loving the children, about demanding sexual favours, about not caring where the food is coming from, about being responsible for the increase in teenage crime and alienation. This collusion may be partly accidental or it may be a shared belief that 'bad men' should suffer. However it came about, it is generating a new kind of error and new forms of pain, all amplified in the name of 'family values'.

The worst thing about this new variation on the old theme of family distress is not the repetition. It is more that all the energy that could go into establishing alternatives is burnt away in the fire-zone of ill-feeling and isolation that comes with exile and loss. No one is suggesting that men not play and pay. But why the accompanying sense that divorce is a sign of a failed life and that an ideal has been failed? Whose ideal? My experience teaches me that marriage takes courage and strength and that divorce takes courage and strength. What seems to be the general opinion is that marriage is some kind of blessing, and separation a sign of failure. Does nobody remember the historical lesson about divorce (especially for women) – that it might bring release and development? Why might that not include children? And a vital chance to build alternatives that work has been lost, replaced in some dreadful version of Nietzsche's idea of 'eternal recurrence' by an endless repeat with different characters in different positions in the same exhausted play.

Last thoughts. The economic future will be determined by forces larger than national governments can manage, and one way the state recognises its weakness is to pull out of areas of social support that it once financed. The family is being asked in that very specific situation to do things it cannot do, and only conservative ideologies dispute this. Some of the arrangements and alternatives put together by the opponents of current state thinking actually have health and flexibility and need support and not moral condemnation. The true anxiety about the family is whether or not these alternatives can be allowed to grow and the focus of attention turned elsewhere on to genuinely frightening things – nuclear, criminal, environmentally degrading. Some of the primitive and pre-bourgeois family forms being built may have the strength to hold up in the future where other familial structures do not. It is a real anxiety as to when if ever this will be admitted, and when the dead will awaken.

Bibliography

P. Laslett and R.Wall, *Household and Family in Past Time*, Cambridge University Press, 1972.

Ferdinand Mount, *The Subversive Family*, Cape, 1982.

Linda Pollock, *Forgotten Children,* Cambridge University Press, 1983.

Lawrence Stone, *The Family, Sex and Marriage in England: 1500–1800*, Weidenfeld & Nicolson, 1977.

Lawrence Stone, *Road to Divorce: England 1530–1987*, Oxford University Press, 1990.

Judith Walkowitz, *City of Dreadful Delight: Narratives of Sexual Danger in Late Victorian London*, Virago, 1992.

Fred D'Aguiar

The Last Essay About Slavery

I have tried to imagine without success a last poem, a last play, a last novel, a last song, about slavery: final acts of creativity in this given area that would somehow disqualify any future need to return to it in these forms. The will to write such a thing is itself a call for slavery to be confined to the past once and for all; for slavery's relevance to present anxieties about race to come to an end; to kill slavery off.

Perhaps I am suffering from slavery-fatigue – a condition brought about by slavery's direct bearing on how the races fail to get along today – to such a degree that I wish it were not so. After many years of reading and listening to slavery's songs, stories and arguments, I want it to have had such an impact on this racially over-determined present that the present becomes cured of a need for it and it can finally be laid to rest.

The Last Novel About Slavery (One Beginning)

A man and a woman are in a tilted field with dozens more men, women and children. They are all chopping or picking their way from one end to the other. Behind them a sun is falling fast, too ashamed to shine on these people in this field. If it could choose, it would never shine in this time again. The woman and the man know it. They feel its shame on their backs. They pray without moving their lips for night to fall. For the light to fail until they can no longer see their hands and the crop in front, always in front, of them. Then they can fall into a deep sleep in one another's arms, too tired to do much more than hug. True or false?

But the present, not slavery, refuses to allow slavery to go away. This present insists that however many stories and arguments about slavery it consumes from writers and singers it still hungers for more. Conditions in the present are not ameliorated by the accumulation of a library of slave-novels, poems, plays, films and albums (cds) about slavery. On the contrary, each generation of blacks demands more of the past. Not because they are suffering short-term memory loss or some such syndrome (after all, didn't the generation before have lots to say about slavery) but because they need their own versions of the past, to see the past in their own images, words. To have slavery nuanced their way.

The Last Novel About Slavery (Another Beginning)

I was born another's property. Named in a ledger as such.

Like my father and his father before him. More than likely is the fact that I will be given a name, several names will summon me and, though I have a given name, I must answer to them all or suffer. But I will die. Propertyless. Another's property. Like my father. And his father before him.

One side of the present refuses to listen to another word about slavery (fed-up whites and embarrassed/ahistorical blacks) so puts up more resistance to it. These recalcitrant blacks have a selective amnesia when it comes to slavery, or else they remember but believe this horrible past cannot be relevant to their problematic present. Does O.J. Simpson believe he is descended from slaves? I don't think he has given it much thought. Does Clarence Thomas? I don't believe he cares about it. Yet both men by their peculiar behaviours exhibit symptoms of shame associated with a slave past. Each may have banished slavery from his mind, but the bodies of both continue to be read in public debate as black and slave-descended. For both men, slavery is not a source of pride, because they are unable to conceive of slavery other than as a source of shame. For both of them, far from slavery being a resource for tackling today's ills, they view it as historical baggage to be jettisoned, irrelevant narratives that serve only to make them look bad in the eyes of their white competitors.

These blacks – and they are to be found in all age-groups, gender and class categories – unwittingly become enablers of white racism, facilitators of the race-hate directed at them. This is historical denial on a grand scale, an invidious form of self-oppression. By withdrawing themselves from the past they leave themselves wide open to racist attack. By seeing a black present as somehow unconnected to past forms of black life, they deposit a damaging aspect of white racism in their psyche: they feed the neurotic myth that they must start from scratch in their search for strategies to combat racism.

O.J. Simpson, like Clarence Thomas before him, is generally regarded as a black man who has elevated himself out of the quagmire of black underachievement and into the arena of white privilege. As such, he is a source of pride for the race, an untouchable as far as criticism is concerned, since there are too few such emblems of pride available to blacks. His trial for double murder was viewed as an attempt to destroy a source of black pride; yet another attack on a successful black. Blacks seemed reluctant to pronounce publicly on his guilt despite overwhelming evidence pointing in that direction, largely because they felt the system could construct any narrative it pleased to destroy blacks since it was white-owned and white-run and in the service of promoting white master-narratives. Blacks felt obliged to support Simpson because they couldn't trust the corrupt system to be fair with a black celebrity. Enter detective Mark Fuhrman as if in confirmation of all those suspicions. A good example of precisely why everything presented as evidence against O.J. Simpson could easily have been fabricated by any number of Mark Fuhrmans attached to the investigation. This neurotic form of reasoning has a basis in American reality all right, but what is astounding is its immovable nature in the face of unstoppable logic. The evidence, along with Detective Mark Fuhrman's compromised testimony, became part of what Clarence Thomas called – in his trump card, last-ditch attempt to save his supreme court nomination against Anita Hill's charges of sexual harassment – a 'high-tech lynch mob'.

When race and gender squared off, as was the case with Clarence Thomas and Anita Hill, race trumped gender (at least in the eyes of blacks). In other words, even if Thomas was wrong and Hill right, given the unfavourable conditions for blacks in the USA, race had to be supported over gender. While many blacks saw through Thomas's cynical use of his race to suit his desperate situation and they were critical of him for playing that race card, they still supported him over Hill. Many whites who were opposed to his candidacy on the ground that he was unqualified for the job backed away in case the racist label attached itself to them. Thomas benefited on both fronts though tarnished by Hill's testimony. The battle-lines were unconventional for American politics. Instead of the usual black/white divide, lines were drawn along gender and ideology. Many women, black and white, supported Hill. And many men and women who held traditional Republican beliefs endorsed Thomas on the grounds that he was a Republican first and a black second, a phenomenon still viewed as an anomaly in US politics, though less so with the Gulf War hero General Colin Powell's high profile consideration late in 1995 to enter the Republican leadership contest.

Simpson's victims were white. Statistically, a black man without Simpson's wealth would have fried in the electric chair on half the evidence (or by firing squad if he were tried in Utah and elected to die that way). Simpson did what the rich do when they are in deep trouble: he assembled a dream-team of lawyers. Everyone witnessed on television how the trial usurped the usual dosage of daytime soap operas and replaced them with the soap opera of real-life court television; they witnessed how American jurisprudence as it stands right now is entirely open to manipulation by the right kind of expertise, available only to the very wealthy.

The jury's verdict, astounding as it still seems, was

inevitable given Simpson's defence team's levelling of the charge of white racism against the Los Angeles Police Department (LAPD) once Fuhrman's racist remarks in those famous tape recordings became admissible evidence. Mark Fuhrman became the harbinger of the notion of reasonable doubt; that somehow, given his negative views of blacks, he had a motive to tamper with the evidence. Even if they believed in Simpson's guilt, the jury disliked the fact that at least one racist in a position of influence had a vested interest in seeing Simpson convicted. In addition, those jurors gathered with the residual knowledge from that first acquittal of Rodney King's attackers, despite the evidence of videotape and a long list of lesser publicised cases of the LAPD's unlawful practices in its dealings with blacks. Never mind the greater interest of justice, that became subverted to the emotive one of race. From Day One of the trial, the LAPD was seen as untrustworthy. By Day One Hundred and Fifty-Four, it was more guilty than Simpson. In an American context this is not surprising. What is sad is that the victims remain without justice as their rights are sacrificed for some misconceived notion of the greater good of the race under attack. The problem with that view is that a probable murderer who happens to be black is at large and the system has been shamed by wealth, by race-based politics and by a history of illegal applications of the law by the LAPD.

Both the Thomas and Simpson cases owe their underlying skewed narratives of what constitutes the facts to a deeper, even more disturbed past when all narratives were tampered with and contorted into one shape, one ideology, namely that of white superiority based on the enslavement of blacks. Under these circumstances, objectivity cannot be assumed in any party or presumed to reside in any institutional process whose foundations were laid at that time. Murderers can walk from a court of law just as sexual harassers can be endorsed as judges in the highest court of the land. With race as a part of the story, the narrative turns out topsy-turvy. Ultimately, though, victims remain victims without recourse to the law and victors never really lose, however pyrrhic their victory.

The Last Novel About Slavery (A Middle)

This is a fact of my heritage. So how can it be over? How can it ever be conferred to a condition of non-being when it lived, still lives, in me? And not just in me. In the names of streets, in the graveyards, in the literature of public and private libraries, in the very architecture that stores these books, my records (at least of when I was born) are reminders of this past, this present, this future, this slavery.

So I choose to forget, to ignore all these daily reminders, these emblems of slavery, and I find a part of me is erased. Forgetting this past because it is negative on the whole, far from restoring me to a weightless sense of the present, denies that present, and robs me of a crucial aspect of itself, and therefore myself. The past is me; I am it. What a terrible past. But it shaped me. What a phoney present to pretend that past did not exist or is somehow over and therefore irrelevant to it. By ignoring that past, I am being ignored.

White supremacists who embrace slavery find that their views of blacks as descendants of slaves make them worthy recipients of white scorn and discrimination. They were inferior then, so the reasoning goes, therefore they qualify to be inferior now. Slavery is used by racists to bludgeon any arguments advanced by blacks about the equality of the races. Their argument maintains that not only have blacks been damaged psychologically by hundreds of years of slavery and only just over a century of freedom, they have been changed genetically, too, made inferior by slavery, suited to their status as second-class citizens, qualified down to their genes for oppression. The obverse is taken as self-evident for these whites who see themselves as descendants of masters and therefore born to rule.

As a result of this dual opposition to history by both parties, past and present continue to validate each other by a process of default. Blacks in trying to forget slavery strenuously validate their need to become acquainted with their past. Racist whites deliberately invoke slavery as an instance from history that justifies turning back (black) the clock of institutional racism.

The last poem, the last play, the last novel and essay about slavery, all have to be redone by each generation: even finality is subject to rehearsals. For example, in Jonestown, Guyana, in November 1978 Jim Jones rehearsed the final calamity of poisoning his nearly 1,000-strong followers with cyanide-laced Kool Aid so frequently that when these so-called 'white nights' become the real and final dark night, his followers had become so numb they were unable to distinguish between the two. Each generation inherits an anxiety about slavery, but the more problematic the present, the higher the anxiety and the more urgent their need to attend to the past. What the anxiety says is quite simply that the past is our only hope for getting through this present. So we return to memory, imagined and real, fanciful and mythical, psychological and genetic: forms of imagination that seek to exorcise the destructive forces of white racism combined with the anxiety and neurosis generated by the negative connotations of a black skin.

The Last Play About Slavery

Two slaves are in the cane- or cotton-fields of a plantation in the Caribbean or United States at the beginning of the nineteenth century. They are working side by side, in silence. They have songs they can sing, but they are saving them for a more appropriate occasion than this, one of forced labour for another. It is dusk, the light is failing fast.

1st slave: *Massa day nearly done.*
2nd slave: *Yes, massa day nearly done.*

The founder of African-American modern thought, W.E.B. DuBois, *(The Souls of Black Folk)* wrote as long ago as 1901: 'The problem of the twentieth century is the problem of the color-line – the relation of the darker to the lighter races.' For 'darker' and 'lighter', read black and white. Any look by a writer at race relations over the last quarter of this century, however cursory, involves a cluster of issues: belonging and alienation; articulations of 'otherness' and 'outsiderness'; imaginative leaps and declarations of communal oneness and sameness; together these provide a reasonable assessment of the truth or falsehood of DuBois' statement.

But there is another index, another way of measuring DuBois' colour-line test against the last twenty-five years – that of the arts, black arts in particular, since they seek to define a problem of being in British society and celebrate a particular brand or expression of humanity. Music and fiction, poetry, the visual arts and drama have addressed the DuBois conundrum, in explicit ways.

DuBois had just witnessed the end of a century dominated by slavery. To DuBois' mind it would take the entire twentieth century to exorcise slavery in all its permutations and new manifestations despite its official death in the courts.

The last twenty-five years in Britain and the USA have confirmed that race issues are central to British and American definitions of themselves, if only because of the pain of witnessing a denial by most whites of this aspect of their sense of nationhood. Look at the many 'birth of a nation' narratives on both sides of the Atlantic and notice the absence of blacks in them, an absence that is so glaring it morphs into an unseen presence or fault-line running through the narrative.

A black contribution, a black experience, a black perspective and a black aesthetic, the articulation of all these has always been a part of literature by whites. But the marginality of blacks in these narratives only confirmed their presence to bolster the stature of whites. Blacks by their very presence or absence make whites look better.

Early black literature (principally the US slave narratives with a few from England) bore witness to a black presence as social and economic victims, because enslaved, but as moral and ethical victors on a quest for freedom. The spiritual well-being of the nation would reside in a repairing of this wrong. Otherwise moral decay would continue and eventually lead to a collapse of the social and economic order.

Black music, from the early black spirituals to blues and jazz, continued to phrase these woes and call for the nation to begin to heal itself by attending to the lot of black people. Part of the lament was celebratory, too: that, despite everything, an essential humanity could not be diminished. I still get a thrill from listening to Bessie Smith's encomiums to her unappeased sexual appetite: man-trouble plagued her, it seems, more than trouble with the Ku Klux Klan! The Klan couldn't be bargained with, it was a given, but at least she could reform her men, through song and by example in her sexual proclivities.

Contemporary black music (mostly reggae, although the odd soul singer and funk band, rap artist and dub poet have occasionally touched on the theme) has embraced a slave heritage to show what blacks experienced and continue to experience in their dealings with despotic power (white or black) and a racist and poverty-generating political system (run by any despot with a stake in it). Part of the vitality of reggae music of the 1970s is its preoccupation with the origins and history of black people. Reggae lyrics embraced difficulty by tackling a history dominated by slavery. It could have gone the way of funk and disco and opted for the escapism of freaking out and partying. Instead it worked through slavery as a direct way to evaluate the current conditions of blacks in the west.

The argument says that in order to understand why blacks are second-class citizens – why they are among the poorest, the most unemployed or underemployed, the most likely to go mad, become criminalised, commit homicide, underachieve in schools, experience police brutality, occupy the lower echelons of all aspects of work skills, tend toward the low zero rather than the high ten on the scale of the powerful, wealthy, admired and well-connected – it is necessary to know the history of blacks in Britain, the Caribbean, the USA and Canada. And since that history, that past, is overwhelmingly dominated by slavery, an examination of how the two races interacted – when those early relations took root to survive into the present times – should lead to solutions for these present problems. I wouldn't dream of using Britain's past to beat up its present – that would be draconian; what I am utilising is a past that has survived into the present, thereby qualifying for inclusion in any critique of the present. An examination of a British and US slave past seeks to understand present-day conflicts between the races.

The songs – from Bob Marley's alternative mythologising in 'Redemption Song' to Burning Spear's feisty celebration of past organisation and resistance in the form of 'Marcus Garvey' – serve as a legacy for today's youth. Though they suffer a little from mythic inflation, nevertheless they achieve a degree of historical recovery that makes the history a felt and living entity, qualities previously unknown to those names and facts. This history would otherwise remain buried in a fusty research library; asleep as closed books. These songs make it possible to hear a painful history as hurt but, in addition, to feel it as a cure, since repeated hearings rehearse the facts as pain which leads to an understanding, which in turn makes it tolerable in a way it could never have been rehabilitated before without the catharsis of song.

Since slavery in the popular mind is associated with a shameful aspect of black history, so the telling of that shame, its airing, is aimed at ameliorating that shame. The songs seem to say, 'we went through all that and we're still here, surviving and fighting'. These songs are testaments, not of the weakness of black people, as the shame about slavery seemed to say, but of black people's obvious strength to have survived all that. Cure resides in knowing the facts and rehabilitating the pain associated with them. And by a trick of the mind brought about by the agency of art, that pain becomes a source of pride and strength. The lyrics are coupled to music born out of a black experience. In other words, history is mediated by a black invention – blues, jazz, reggae, funk, soul. Furthermore, these inventions are at the heart of that struggle to define a black heritage during a post-itis (the malady of post-everything) age.

Stories are at the heart of these rehearsals of the facts of the past. Marley's 'Redemption Song' tells a story. Burning Spear's 'Marcus Garvey' awakens the listener to the existence of a figure from recent Caribbean history who laid the foundations back in the 1920s and 1930s for a Black Power movement in the 1960s to mid-1970s. But the stories do more: they resurrect these historical artifacts and make them 'real' to a majority of people, not just a post-graduate few. Part of this 'reality' in, say, 'Redemption Song', is that it makes a connection between the past and present by drawing a narrative arc from the distant past to the present in a simple story-telling form and in the language of everyday speech. Yet Marley is able to work history as if it were myth by drawing out its symbols. His tone appears to speak to everyone and the themes he explores are understood almost at the level of intuition though clearly engaged with history. 'Marcus Garvey' talks about a 1920s and 1930s struggle by going backwards to slave-times and moving forwards to 1970s Jamaica and black people's struggle in all modern societies for a positive self-image to replace the negative definitions of themselves. It argues too for self-empowerment.

In addition, both Marley and Burning Spear invoke an idealised geography, one that predates the deracination of slavery, namely Africa. The return is metaphorical, not literal (though Garvey's 'Black Star Liner' seemed to work against metaphor, Burning Spear's lyrics do not), and in terms of heritage. What is acknowledged is a separation from Africa and a need to reconnect with it by fostering an Africa-centred consciousness. British reggae bands such as Steel Pulse, Aswad and Misty in Roots argue as much in their lyrics. Their songs re-create the journey of the slave triangle to show not discontinuity and fracture, but survival and repair, not forgetting and alienation but the triumph of memory and community. An unwritten feminist perspective in that middle passage is in need of expression if the artistic expression is to match the historical reality. These constructs of a psychic bridge to Africa, these re-makings of the journey of the middle passage, attempt to locate black people in Europe armed with an unviolated – because pre-slavery – sense of self with which to combat British racism. Of course this model is replete with problems, the biggest being that of Africa's own culpability in the slave system even before a European involvement, but that's another matter. What's critical for any consideration of our neurotic present is that Africa becomes a part of the myth of history – that process of the imaginative constructing of a past to replace one that has been scrambled in the memory.

Fiction of the last quarter-century has followed this lead. Rather than exhausting a theme as another writer working at the seam of slavery, I find mine inexhaustible; it appears to deliver up further possibilities for exploration. It is as though each articulation, each imagining, feeds the need for a further act of retrieval. In fiction as in song, the story continues both to bring to life a past that might otherwise remain lost or distorted into shame, and to convert that past from pain to cure.

Race riots and institutionalised racism (though together they make damning testimony) are an insufficient basis for testing DuBois. What is required is a return to slavery (a going back to the past in order to get to the future), to history, to Stephen Daedalus's nightmare from which he arguably never woke: that is, the genesis of these spoiled relations between black and white, as seen in novels about slavery by writers from both races.

Certain questions are raised by this imaginative act of looking back. People question its relevance. Why write another slave novel? In other words: Hasn't it been done to death? Or, why write one *now*? That is, who needs such misery in this mean time? This view sees slave novels as counter-productive because they remind an ugly present of an even uglier antecedent – the past. They feel vindicated in their opposition to this tendency of writers to delve into slavery when they ask such questions as: Where are the remedies in these novels for problems between the races? And, what, if any, useful social policies can we extract from them? Or, how can a long spell of black people in defeat possibly contribute to the dire need to bolster black pride? Even, why should white people be humbled by stories in which they are unremitting winners, albeit cruel ones? And they get answers like, any explanation of why the impulse is there to write stories about slavery resides in the novels themselves. But the fact remains that ideas about slavery are buried in the deliberations and experiences of characters who inhabit that world. These characters and their experiences *are* their own rationale. What is clear from reading novels about slavery and writing one myself (and this response is true for readers of other kinds of stories) is that 'things' happen to all witnessing readers that affect their view of themselves and of the multi-racial world they inhabit. One of these effects is emotional: readers find that their coveted maps of empathy are redrawn by their engagement with these slave novels; redrawn in terms of their ability to experience fellow-feeling for someone of a different race, the opposite gender and the power-brokered relationships between and within such groupings. Readers emerge emotionally bruised, mentally reconfigured and, as a consequence, with a deeper knowledge of those relations.

Writing about slavery affords a similar perspective. I

was surprised by the twists and turns the story took once the characters started to think and interact around a given dilemma. As the novel grew, so did the complexities of the lives involved. It was impossible to draw DuBois' colour-line in terms of character, since each character shared with the other similar traits even as their dreams were circumscribed by different realities depending on race. What concerned them then seems to concern me and others engaged with the subject now: not the same circumstances, but the same worries. That skin should continue to carry a high premium and not character. That asseveration to race as a category overrules all other groupings. That even in the arts of the imagination race refuses to be transcended.

The Last Novel About Slavery (One Ending Out Of Many Possible Endings)

I have found love after a hard life. To be frank, I doubted such love ever existed in this world. All I could see and all that was handed to me were the many opposites of love. What else in this mean world has as many opposites as love, as many varieties and variations on those opposites? So many that one expression has dreamed up chains for me, a life of forced labour for me, the auction block for me and, for sport, castration.

But I am one of the lucky ones. I lived long enough to have found love. Actually, I did not recognise love at first. When love waltzed up to me, I mistook her for pity. And, since I hate being pitied, I was angry and gave her such rebuttals that I am surprised she is still here.

But love must have surmised a great need in me for her. Love persisted. She persisted. Though I recoiled from her touch, reviled her for ever wanting to touch – of all hated things and abused manifestations on this earth – me.

Now I can't get enough of love. Of love's touch. Her smile. Now, when I walk past a mirror, I see a man looking back. (Not a boy, not a mule, not a nigger.) And that man is me.

For black readers, history is recovered in fiction. A history of unwritten lives that was previously lost to them is suddenly revealed. This contemporary fictional history is different in tone and register from the slave narratives, many of them ghost-written, of the day. The indignities of slavery are re-created by these fictions as though they were actual narratives but with fiction's added ability to ironise, to ennoble and dignify the demeaned life, the dehumanised slave, by recovering their humanity, but with an ironic detachment afforded by the privilege of retrospective wisdom and of art. Whereas in the slave narrative the life of the slave is the subject of the story that the reader is privileged to overhear, in the slave novel that life is rendered in such a way that the reader becomes the subject, no longer able to sit outside it as witness but put in its place. The reader becomes both the 'thing' doing the talking and the 'thing' talked about in slave novels: not a single entity but splintered; not in one fixed location or vantage-point but shifting.

Faulkner's dictum that the past is never past, because it is always parading as the present, neatly positions the past and the present on a continuum. It means that past dilemmas can never be set aside and that the impact of the past on the present is such that an examination of the past can lead to the discovery of solutions for present-day dilemmas.

When writers ransack the history of slavery for its emblems, for the art of the hurt, they are, in essence, engaged in a search for stories, for character, and for events. The act of looking back not only acknowledges the present in the past, it admits, too, the future in the past. The descendants of slaves are hurting because the present isn't working for them. They are shackled to a past by the failure of the present (the recent present) to examine that past in a way that makes sense as rhetoric, as emblem, as art. It is not enough to direct someone to the large body of research on slavery as a means to assuage that hurt. A vocabulary is needed to furnish the custom-made emblems that cope with pain. Each generation demands something different from those stories, some shift in emphasis or focus, some alteration in tone and nuance, that has a direct bearing on the ease of their own inherited hurt.

The talent to articulate a black experience (because it is framed by art) is not the sole preserve of black artists. The question concerns the degree of artistry of the expression. All the truths and insights and emotional impact of the expression, the experience-as-art that is being written, depend on the efficacy of this artistry. And since the endowment of imagination has no regard for race, sex, gender or class, any artist can render a black experience as successful – because persuasive – art.

This is part of the power of the story. In essence it denies the exclusivity of any one group or individual experience. It seeks to communicate against that privatising zeal in us all, that impulse to say: 'This is mine and no one else's.' It posits ways of linking one person to the next, one strange group to another, by revealing aspects thought exclusive to one as resident in the other, and by showing difference as bridgeable.

The story has no loyalties even as it simmers in the particular soup of its time. Like the Nobel Laureate Derek Walcott's lonely emissary in his long autobiographical poem, 'Another Life', it boasts, 'I have no friends but words.' Of course it is prone to amateur dramatics, to high camp – the Liberace of art forms – unless governed by restraint and a certain ironic distancing by the writer. It will sell its mother to achieve its goal: hijacking the reader intellectually and emotionally for the ransom of persuading that reader of its point of view.

My brand of slave novel is more contemporary in its phrasing, more conscious of saying something to the reader about now as much as about then, and more poetic. By poetic, I mean a deliberate reaching-up or elevation in the tone of the narration and a preponderance of suggestive imagery which takes the place of the usual scene-setting detail.

The future for this kind of writing is not finite. Each new book exposes new possibilities ripe for exploration. Slavery presents itself as an inexhaustible seam precisely because of its relevance to the contemporary scene. The continuous hurt of slavery rests in the fact that a mere knowledge of it is enough to cause pain. Without fiction, this history would remain a source of anger and grief without any hope or ability to transcend them, except through amnesia, which is the end of hope.

To doubt the validity of their existence is to wish history would come to an end. To murder history in this way is to commit a crime against the present, since the present consists largely of the past. Books about slavery are living things. Closed books are asleep; open books awake as readers. It is this life of slavery that is being contested. Some people want it dead. They want to kill memory; kill its capacity to live as stories. How can memory be threatened with homicide when it died long ago as living testimony? Because it has re-emerged as imagination.

If these contemporary novels were to disappear, there would be a massive absence of eloquence about slavery. These stories belie any notion of the past being past. In fact they prove, through character, the presence of the past and perhaps even the past in the future. Mexico's premier poet, Octavio Paz, said, 'our greatest enemy is history.' In this instance history is our greatest ally in shaping the future.

The Last Sonnet About Slavery

(*After paintings by Hogarth*)

Put your hand on my shoulder, dear mistress.
Hands as delicate should not hang in the air
But find ample places to pose and rest.
And since my shoulders, my head, the hair
On it, all belong to you, let those hands
Settle anywhere on me, but do not let them float
Aimlessly, nor be idle, nor stand
Out as if they had no greater goal.

Hands that don't know the scrubbing brush,
Or weight of any thing, other than a necklace
Or dress, stocking or shift that they adjust,
Are not hands, but butterflies on a leash.
Let them wave and dart if you must, but please,
When they settle, let their good luck fall on me.

Did DuBois get it right? His vision of the century

omitted the growth of gender politics. He did not foresee the rise and fall of class politics. Neither did he allow for the savage excesses of the Holocaust, though it too can be admitted as part of a race war. What about the twenty-first century? Does his colour-line spill over into it like a long shadow throughout its wide span? I fear so; I hope not. I'd invoke King's dream of little black and white children living in a kind of Coca Cola (sugar-free and caffeine-free, though still lip-smacking, thirst-quenching) harmony.

If anything, DuBois' binary opposition is too simplistic for the age: it does not account for a Clarence Thomas who appears to cross that line, when it comes to the acquisition of power, and become invisible (after everything that the protagonist in Ellison's 'Invisible Man' went through to win his visibility!) but who can also contract into the collective history of hurt of his race at will as demonstrated by that notorious phrase of his, to evade substantial charges of verbal sexual abuse. Colour is compounded by poverty, by class, by gender. Rich and powerful blacks can elevate themselves out of the strictures put upon poor blacks. Freeing themselves of all the negative attachments that go with a dark skin, they are transformed by power and money into honorary whites. Black women face the same acts of chauvinism from men, black or white, since the impact is the same, damaging and unwanted.

A multi-faceted rubric is needed now: one that draws on myth and landscape; that finds examples of a complex multi-racial community in the New World or on the margins of the old. Such a model would show not just division, but allegiances across race, class and sex boundaries. Conflict continues between the categories, but with the possibility of renewal for an Old World much in need of these new figurations.

The Last Poem About Slavery

1

A whip is a light thing
until it lands on skin.

Then it's hot and heavy.

2

Someone, somewhere beat me
and someone with my looks,

sometime, so long, so bad,

that the mere thought of whips
tenses, welts our bodies.

3

The whip is not to blame.

Beautiful in its way,
air and body are platforms

for a performance;

blame that director's hand
and producer's desire.

4

There is more to slavery
than a whip, quip and slip.

A model of race as a plural notion, steeped in

community and landscape and reliant on past and present myths alongside past or present histories rather than the dangerous essentialism of identity politics, takes us deep into the twenty-first century. Knowing this, I feel better about going there. My journey is being made not simply as a black man, but with my blackness as one vital component among a set of complex related conditions (class, gender, politics, and capacities for love and creativity, to name some) that are not fixed but shifting, and subject to visions and revisions.

Susie Orbach

Couching Anxieties

Anxious: troubled in mind, XVII century stem anx- of *angere*, choke, oppress. **Anxiety:** uneasiness of mind, XVI century.

Joke: If you are anxious you need to see an analyst. If you aren't anxious you *definitely* need to see an analyst.

It's a funny old discipline – psychoanalysis. Not so old, really, just over a hundred years. But in that time it has developed from a clinical practice into a theory of mind, a cultural critique, a leading contributor to literary studies, the partner of branches of modern philosophy and gender studies. Today, psychoanalysis is stretched by the demands upon it, by the fantasies of what it can provide, by the accusations laid at its door:

'It's a palliative for modern ills'

> 'It's the soft cop, resocialising justified social rage into the management of personal pain'
>
> 'It made women in the fifties and sixties feel that their distress was their own inadequacy'
>
> 'It's about denying the reality of child sexual abuse focusing instead on the phantasy'
>
> 'It's about insinuating that there has been sexual abuse where none exists'
>
> 'It makes people self-involved, zaps their energy'
>
> 'A modern relationship without therapy is hell'
>
> 'Psychoanalysis is part of the socialist conspiracy which enervates initiative and creates a culture of dependency'
>
> 'Psychoanalysis is all about letting people off the hook, understanding and forgiving them for everything'
>
> 'Psychoanalysis is subversive'
>
> 'Psychoanalysis is indispensable to understanding the reproduction of patriarchy.'

Psychoanalysis is all things to all people.

Psychoanalysis, like politics, science and religion, contains within it tendencies and practices that are diametrically opposed to each other. From its beginnings, psychoanalysis, both as theory and as a clinical practice, has embodied conflicting tendencies, conflicting understandings of the contents of the psyche, and conflicting views on its application outside of the clinic. Depending upon its context and who has been proposing it, psychoanalysis has been employed in reactionary and progressive ways. This is as true now as it was at the turn of the century.

When some feminists[1] took up psychoanalysis as a way of understanding gender relations and the reproduction of femininity in the early 1970s, it caused a furore within the Women's Liberation Movement. Partly this was because the history of the progressive use of psychoanalysis had been lost,[2] and partly it was because of psychoanalysis' conservative, normalising role in the United States in the fifties. Betty Friedan's critique of psychoanalysis' resocialising of female angst and the Radical Therapy Movement's concern that psychotherapy and psychoanalysis were powerful tools for the silencing of socially constructed pain and madness meant that psychoanalysis was inevitably greeted with suspicion.

Coming from the New Left, being British and raised in a climate in which Freudian ideas weren't given much credence, I too was suspicious. Indeed, I was initially unreceptive to psychoanalytic ideas. But my experience in America of teaching women's studies in a working-class college in 1970 with strong links to its local community on Staten Island, and observing female faculty and students attempting to transform their lives changed my mind. It suggested to me that one needed more texture to explain women's continued acceptance of their own subordination once economic factors had been removed. I was drawn, along with many friends and colleagues, to ask the question: How it was that women could be so deeply committed to do what was not in their best interest. I observed that doing what felt 'in their best interests' was so anxiety-provoking that, even within the groundswell of a movement which provided significant social support, women found it difficult to reverse situations of discontent. Again and again, women in the Women's Liberation Movement were asking themselves questions that had first been asked within the left: What is the meaning and impact of the consciousness we hold? Where do our ideas come from? How do ideas that we no longer believe in still incline us to act in certain ways? Why do we act so seemingly irrationally? What is this thing called socialisation? How profound is it? Does it reach into the very construction of who we are? Why, when life is economically, socially and politically unbalanced, do those who are disadvantaged co-operate? Why do we sanction a system so obviously not in our interests?

I make these remarks, and remember these questions, to take us back to the origins of my interest in psychoanalysis as an accompaniment to political endeavour. For many of my generation, the generation of 1968, these questions could begin to be answered by a new addition to the discussion: a way of understanding, thinking and looking at human behaviour that amplified the economic and sociological analyses of the day. Psychoanalysis, with its inclusion of the unconscious, is a window into understanding the inter- and intra-psychic process of the human being and, by so doing, reformulates the question.

The appropriation of psychoanalysis to left causes was nothing new. As Russell Jacoby[3] has so beautifully detailed, the *Rundbriefe* that circulated around Otto Fenichel and other politically committed psychoanalysts in the thirties and forties was part of what some psychoanalysts saw as the politically subversive potential of this new discipline.

Outside the clinic, the Frankfurt School used psychoanalytic ideas to understand the collapse of social democracy and the installation of fascism in Germany. And yet, despite a history of association with radical ideas and movements almost as long as the history of psychoanalysis itself, psychoanalysis within Britain, within political circles, even within the editorship of this book, has had to make the legitimacy of its argument over and over again.

I want to write about what, from my perspective, psychoanalysis has let us see and understand. And I want to write not what specific policies psychoanalysis would fight for, but to talk about how psychoanalytic ways of thinking refresh the political in useful ways, adding a dimension of understanding to political issues that is absent in our present programmatic approach to issues.

Given ten minutes to talk to the Labour front bench about psychoanalysis and legislation, there is no quick fix, no manifesto, no what is to be done. Psychoanalysis like other discourses is not a political practice, although it can be political in its application and political within its practice. Psychoanalysis does not convert into a set of programmes. However psychoanalytic perspective on contemporary problems is invaluable in thinking through, with other expert disciplines, how one might, if one were legislating, make it possible for certain desired outcomes to occur. How can psychoanalysis do this?

Freud, Janet, Breuer and other workers at the frontier of the new science of human feeling and behaviour imbibed the spectacular successes of nineteenth-century science and medicine, creating a sensibility within which Freud and his contemporaries felt that it was possible to begin to understand human subjective experience. If the wonders of the natural world could be understood, the place of the human being, the actions of the human being, the motivation of the human being, the passions of the human being, the interactions between human beings, might also be comprehensible. The human being as subject was no longer to be the sole province of literature, art or religion – disciplines that were descriptive rather than analytic. The new discipline of psychoanalysis took as its project human mental life. It strove to understand what motivates the individual and the group. By the turn of the century, psychoanalysis became a central part of the modernist project which has sought to understand the natural and physical world as well as the social, economic and emotional worlds that human beings in the west inhabit.

For many today however, the modernist project is a nonsense. In surveying a century which includes the industrialisation of killing in the most civilised centres of western culture, the charge has been laid that modernism and its intellectual components/companions from psychoanalysis to physics have failed. Our cities are replete with degradation, with racism, our countryside devastated by the profligacy that comes from wanton technological production for profit and consumerism. The failure of the modernist project to achieve a world of justice and plenty has led some to argue that the understandings offered by modernist disciplines are either inadequate, impossible in principle, or wrong. In its place, post-modernism has been offering new lenses through which contemporary society and individual behaviour can be viewed. It has found a receptive audience. In these pre-millennium years of malaise, despair, fragmentation and anxiety, a theory of the particular that eschews coherence in favour of fragmentation strikes a compatible note.

But post-modernism isn't fully satisfactory. It often appears to parallel and mimic what it sees rather than extending understanding. While it allows us to handle a multiplicity of agendas, its refusal to order them, or its delight in the disorder, reiterates the fragmentation that characterises our age. The thinking it proposes is itself fractured and incoherent. At its worst, it is a shopping basket of possibilities rather than a deeply thought through understanding of ourselves and our predicament.

I want to argue, against the current intellectual trend to valorise post-modernism, that the modernist project, including contemporary psychoanalysis, is still a very valuable tool for thinking about human beings. Far from being limited to the consulting room, psychoanalysis has much to contribute to contemporary political and cultural concerns. But psychoanalysis is doomed to fail as part of such a project if it is represented as a discourse of the rational. Its strength lies in its ability to tell us about what is insufficient about the rational or, to put it another way, what may be behind the seemingly rational. By giving us ways to think about, explore and contextualise that which seems perverse, bizarre, extraordinary, inexplicable, destructive, counterproductive, we enrich our understanding and thus our capacity for effective action.

Through language and the talking cure, psychoanalysis has found a way to decode and uncover the secrets embedded in the symptoms that patients exhibit. We've learnt that the human animal is a social, interactive, interdependent being who will do almost anything, knit its psyche into the most incredible knots, in order to maintain its relationship with significant others. We've learnt that early experience shapes our responses to self and other, makes the world a benevolent, frightening, overwhelming, welcoming or benign environment. We've learnt that the familial, domestic, cultural, class, financial, religious, ethical background we spring from will be deeply structured into our individual's sense-of-self-determining sets of behaviours. We've learnt that good relationships – those which support individuation and connectedness, embrace vulnerability and strength – allow the individual to feel secure inside themselves and make connections with others based on interest, love and communication. We've learnt that bad relationships – those that hurt rather than empower, disable rather than enable – become a magnet attracting and manacling the individual who has been attached to them, instilling in them an emotional repertoire which inclines them to re-create relationships impregnated with that emotional tableau.

With psychoanalysis, we've learned about human agency, the meanings individuals make out of their circumstances and how those meanings, which are unique, personal and idiosyncratic, represent people's sense of their individuality, their active participation in the making of self: their human agency. Few people feel themselves to be puppets. However devoid of meaning, however depressed, passive and dejected many people are – unless they are driven by voices, which on a good day even they will acknowledge must derive from the self – the sense that they have intention, that they are the actors in their own lives, exists. People may not understand why they always leave their work to the last minute, bite their nails, can't make good relationships, shout at the children, don't know what they want, feel compelled to drink, act powerless and so on, but in a part of their inner experience there resides the idea that they are the authors of their own lives.

As clinicians we've discovered that we can help people to reverse the impact of damaging early experience, although it takes time, patience, great skill and the determination of both parties. We've discovered the human capacity for cruelty. And we discovered the human capacity to deny being a recipient of cruelty by a process in which the victim refashions an understanding of the cruelty in their heads that removes culpability from the perpetrator to the recipient. We've learnt that, when the pain is too great, individuals dissociate. They split off their experience from their conscious awareness and it is banished, frozen, held in unformulated capsules, unelaborated, always threatening exposure. We've learnt that distressing experience gets temporarily relieved by being re-enacted, by the victim taking on the role of the perpetrator and trying both to emulate and to understand the actions of their torturer as well as to understand how they themselves survived. We've understood a great deal, it seems to me, about the psychic mechanisms we employ to manage, assuage and survive. We know what can happen to the individual when aggressed on, the long-term effects, the possible responses. We've learnt enough to know that emotional distress extracts an enormous toll from individuals and the people around them, as well as from the health, social, teaching and economic services.

And just as we regard numeracy, literacy and public health as essential prerequisites for living in our world, so we can begin to consider how to integrate the insights of one hundred years of clinical psychoanalysis into our approach to the world. We can begin to consider how to create the emotional literacy that allows people to feel unafraid of their emotional responses, to process their feelings in ways that extend rather than diminish them, to enable people to tolerate the emotional lives of one another without being so overwhelmed that they wish to silence them. To say that, in British culture, emotional expressiveness has a particular form is not to suggest that we imitate the cultural practices of other more excitable cultures. But it is to look at the social and psychological consequences of repression and how it can disable individuals, families and the wider community. Managing emotional responses as opposed to being frightened of them, would make a great deal of difference to many people's lives. At present we have a situation in which we reward the heroic in emotional life. We sanction explosive emotional states – love, hate, anger. Our cultural pursuits enshrine the grand emotions while we create little space to assimilate either the complexity or the subtlety of much of our emotional responses. We regard vulnerability and helplessness as childish, fear as something to be overcome rather than recognised, emotions as somehow in the way of life rather than a constituent part of what it means to be alive.

What we've learnt so far about how human beings function best, where they have a chance to think, feel, create, initiate, create community, could be fashioned into a document about what human beings require. Obviously the two places to start are the family and the school, and both these institutions have attracted many interventions of late. The circle in school, parenting groups with psychological perspectives, anti-bullying programmes, mediation for parents who are separating, are instances of the kinds of practice that will make emotional literacy a commonplace rather than an uncommon occurrence. The social and economic benefits of children and grown-ups being able to contain and sort through their feelings are considerable. No one doubts this, but the political will to help people to enact such programmes is lacking and many of the efforts rest on voluntary or charitable labour. While Tony Blair wants to talk about linking parental rights with parental responsibility in particular, he has been less able to explain what might be an effective strategy for doing so. Much of British political rhetoric now encompasses a drift to a soft communitarian agenda, where what is supposed to transform social relations is left mysteriously woolly. By contrast, there are scores of programmes, like the list above, whose aim is to raise the level of emotional literacy already in place.[4]

The analytic way of thinking is a direct challenge to modes of exclusion which characterise much of political discourse. Fundamentalism, scapegoating, nostalgia, vigilantism, authoritarianism, compartmentalisation are features of public life today that characterise the discussion of contentious political issues. It is easy to observe that complex issues are often framed in such a way so as to reduce them to a slogan – 'single mothers', 'so-called asylum-seekers', 'welfare chisellers', etc. Political discourse is unused to managing complexity, ambiguity and contradiction. While such a way of thinking is not exclusive to psychoanalysis, nevertheless the management, containment and expression of complexity, ambiguity and contradiction is one of the hallmarks of contemporary psychoanalytic thought and practice, and it is in this arena that psychoanalysis has much to offer towards reframing politics in the age of anxiety.

I'm thinking now of the kind of shift in political discourse that could arise if political concerns and conversations were not afraid to address the complexities of an argument or the anxiety that a difficult situation poses. When we talk of crime or prisons, the conventional political discussion is polarised. The right defines violent criminality as an aberration; as something that belongs to violent criminals. It sees the responsibility as lying with the individual. By removing the contaminated individual, we are free of violence. The liberal sees the violence as inherent in an inequitable system. It is an understandable if unfortunate response to the violence of social deprivation. In one position the individual is all responsible, in the other, there is no individual.

A psychoanalytically informed perspective would recognise that both these positions contain truths and that they are not answers to each other, but are aspects of an answer to a question which both sides are posing: what is to be done about violence and criminality?

Because human beings are inclined to have multiple, contradictory experiences in their development and to process and internalise their parents or carers idiosyncratically, these will be psychologically embodied in complex ways. Good and bad cannot be so conveniently separated and split. It is not that society can just excise its bad bits. Bad bits of society and of individuals are related to the good bits. They exist in relation to one another and are defined by one another. Our rage, violence and destructiveness are not part of the bad bit of ourselves and the loving, caring, apparently altruistic, bit the good bit. Rather, an individual's capacity to be caring can be deconstructed just as can their rage. It may, for example, be that an aspect of an individual's rage at being uncared for creates a defence structure which works to protect the person from unconscious feelings of rage, despair and sense of unentitlement that can occur when needs have gone unrecognised by another. This lack of recognition is internalised by the individual in a complex way. A part of the individual experiences the lack of recognition as a statement of an authentic situation: they are unentitled, unworthy, undeserving. Out of this sensibility, they strive to give to others whom they may unconsciously identify with, thus yielding a sense of vicarious gratification. At the same time, the feelings of unworthiness are assuaged by the conception of self as giving. The giving then is not an act of altruism. It is not even an act of goodness *per se*. It is the psychic expression of a self who wishes to receive, who is confused about his or her entitlement to receive and who may be aggrieved. The giving is an attempt to take care of the self.

As another part of the psychological complexities of rage, crime and violence, we can see an alternative attempted internalisation working in the following way. The experience of not being recognised is unbearable. The person feels angry but is unable to contain that feeling inside her or himself because that too finds no recognition. Feelings of anger then have to be located in another through the process of projection. Others are seen as angry, the self is felt too benign. If the anger is even more impermissible to the self, then it is expelled in the complex process of projective identification – not only is it seen in another but it may be induced in the other. One finds an other or others whose anger is available for stimulation for their own reasons. Once located and evoked in the other, the projector is free of his or her own angry or violent feelings. In other words, society's attempts to split and dissociate that which is violent and bad from that which is good and caring will misfire unless what might underpin either response is understood in terms more complex than simple polarisations.

Psychoanalysis sees the human agency in all human action. To explain a process is not to abdicate responsibility. It doesn't see the individual who is violent as only a victim. It recognises that individuals are both victim and author of their own acts, that while violence begets violence and individuals will enact in the world a version of what they have experienced in their local emotional repertoire, what they enact needs to be decoded, understood and held long enough to be thought about and transformed. If for example, young men in Newcastle[5] feel they exist only if they can act violently against their environment, if trashing it is a means of self-expression and personal agency, what then is the message? The message is of course in part that society has shut them out of participating in the world in a recognisably meaningful way – they have no job prospects, therefore no way to contribute; no money, therefore no way to participate in consumer society; they are excluded. But what psychoanalysis adds is the notion that acts of violence can be attempts at externalising what can't be digested, as well as statements of transformation. The violence conveys the unmetabolised destructiveness felt inside the (excluded) individual and the (excluded) group by rendering that destruction outside. People destroy what has been created as an enactment of the destructiveness lodged inside them. They make visible what is otherwise invisible. They shift the discomfort from inside themselves into the environment, where the devastation becomes inescapable. They draw us into it. What the young men find indigestible is foisted on the environment and made indigestible to us all. It is outside them, facing us. In the process of externalisation the young men gain a sense of power, and we now experience the indigestibility, the unacceptability, the destructiveness of such a life.

It is in this texture of knowing the active human subject that psychoanalysis can add to public debate. Perpetrators of crime and violence are neither victims nor devils but are responding to the facts of their social existence with emotional ranges common to all humanity. This is the kind of understanding that psychoanalysis can bring to the political process. A psychoanalytically-informed discussion of violent crime is a critique of the explanation and solution that depends upon a primitive splitting into bad and good. It demands that we think in more complex categories, that we find ways of managing differing perspectives and contradiction.

I am describing how psychoanalysis can contribute to the political process. I am not describing a party political policy about crime. Nevertheless we can see immediately that any policy that attempts to meet violence with violence is doomed to fail, if not in the short term, then in the long term. Harsh sentencing, brutal prisons, an army-trained probation service, punitive parole officers, speak to the desire to contain and separate out the problem from society. What is required is a different understanding of containment and boundaries, spaces in which those who have come to enact life through violence can engage their bellicosity in ways that begin to deconstruct it rather than reinforce it. To be sure violence is difficult to shift, but it has no chance of being shifted if it is returned in kind by a criminal justice system which enshrines it as a part of practice. A psychoanalytic understanding of the psychological roots of violence, of the structures required to begin to reverse it and thus extend the emotional range of the violent individual needs to be embodied in the solution. Psychoanalysis knows about containment and boundaries, and its under-utilisation in the criminal justice system is foolhardy.

The incorporation of psychoanalytic perspectives into government committees where policy issues were under discussion could make possible an enriched public conversation. The psychoanalyst Andrew Samuels has a vision that places a psychotherapist on policy committees as one of the experts who would routinely advise government. He sees psychotherapists sitting down with the statisticians, economists, taxation experts, social policy advisers to contribute to the conceptualisation of issues and policy formulation. Certainly we can see immediately how the expert panel on violence and crime would be strengthened by a psychotherapist's contributions. My thought is a complementary one. I envision a cabinet minister vested to scrutinise every piece of policy for its emotional, social and political consequences.[6] The team of this minister would perform a psychosocial audit of proposed legislation, assessing its emotional, economic, health and social costs. The consequences of short-term policy initiatives can be hugely disruptive. Sometimes a government will be working to create disruption because that is what is desired; sometimes it will be acting to satisfy an economic gain; sometimes to secure an immediate advantage, to correct policies that are inadequate. Whatever the case, the consequences are not thought through well enough. Our present consultation processes with Green and White Papers go some way to exploring complexity, but the absence of a department actively thinking about the consequences of legislation from multiple perspectives severely limits their usefulness. If the idea alarms us, this itself should give us pause. Because surely we aren't saying that because something is difficult to think through and we might find out adverse consequences we therefore shouldn't think? Is a government to be seen as the now maligned management style of a chief executive of a corporation who is interested only in short-term profit rather than long-term investment?

Placing a psychotherapist as part of the routine consultation process of governmental committees and introducing a department of long-term assessment would extend and expand the political vocabulary and landscape as we know it. The first attempts to make explicit and visible the psychological dimensions in any public issue; the second looks at the consequences to society when emotional issues are being exploited rather than addressed.

This three-pronged intervention into public life – a policy document for emotional literacy, the broadening of political conversation to include complexity and contradiction and the insertion of a depth psychological perspective into policy initiatives – is a necessary part of the remaking of Britain today. Psychoanalysis, in making the unconscious conscious, explores underlying anxieties. Our underlying anxieties about Britain today and what cannot be spoken could, with psychoanalysis' aid, begin to be addressed.

For the best part of a century, denial has been a political tool. The demise of the Empire is still not fully assimilated, even though several generations have grown up since its collapse. The issues of loss, of guilt, of confusion and terror that need to be explored are hijacked by a political discourse that favours nostalgia and racism. The debates about Europe are informed not by a sober consideration of costs and benefits, of the meaning of national identity for the new millennium, about the relationship between separateness and attachment, affiliation and autonomy but by an emotional appeal to nationalism that is exploited by politicians for short-term partisan gain rather than being fully addressed for the benefit of the growth of the nation as a whole. The inability to come to terms with the loss (or the relief of loss) of the Empire is converted into the struggle over Europe and British identity. The problem of incorporating the results of Empire is to shift the ground and create a new other, which threatens to vanquish Britain, a new enemy. The economic and social consequences of Empire, the coming to grips with the transformation of Britain from a wealthy country to a rapidly declining economy can thus remain largely neglected.

For psychoanalysis to be of value in an age of anxiety, it has to explore the personal and social anxieties that beset us. They are interlinked and yet separate. The co-mingling of anxieties makes for a lethal brew. At present the public sphere is a stage for the enactment of private agonies, and the private realm the space for the dumping of socially constructed distress. In psychoanalysis we have a really useful tool that can enable us to think deeply and creatively about the anxieties that beset us today.

Notes

1. e.g. Juliet Mitchell. See for example *British Journal of Psychotherapy*, vol.12, no.1, Symposium on Feminism and Psychoanalysis.
2. Just as the history of the first women's movement had been.
3. Jacoby, R. (1983) *The Repression of Psychoanalysis*, New York, Basic Books.
4. See The Parenting Forum, National Children's Bureau, 8 Wakley Street, London EC1V 7QE.
5. See Beatrix Campbell's *Goliath*, Methuen 1993.
6. The World Health Organisation has introduced a Minister of Consequences on to its environmental committees with the brief to work out the environmental and health consequences of legislation and policy initiatives.

Geoff Watts

Can Science Reassure?

'Religious leaders take on the scientists who would play God' (headline from the *Independent on Sunday,* 4 June 1995)

There was nothing exceptional about the story printed beneath that Sunday headline. It was a speculative piece about the introduction of human genes into pigs, the idea being to make their tissues more compatible with ours, and so boost their potential as a source of organs for transplantation. The *Independent on Sunday* is hardly a tabloid (no 'God squad aim to zap Frankensteins' here), but its story's menu of religious objections to this and other developments in genetic engineering was generously seasoned with words and phrases calculated to bring out a flavour of apprehension. There were the mandatory references to Aldous Huxley and a 'brave new world'; there was discussion of genetic engineers 'engaging in sin', seeking to 'subordinate the ways of God', and designing 'boutique children'; there were suggestions that we are on the 'threshold of mind-bending debates' about the nature of life.

Stories like this are not unusual; the *Independent on Sunday* piece just happened to appear on the day I began thinking about this essay. Which is precisely my point; you don't *have* to search hard for reports which dwell on the 'potentially explosive implications for the human race' of scientific developments. There are scores of them.

The same issue of the same paper carried another science story. Headlined 'Why be so careless with the facts?', it rightly criticised Greenpeace for publishing an advertisement intended to whip up fears about environmental pollution on the surprising grounds that chemicals dumped into the oceans 'are causing our willies to shrink in size'. And the article – as sober in tone as the Greenpeace ad was hysterical – went on to offer other examples of the environmentalists' dubious use of scientific evidence.

Newspapers can mould opinion, or reflect it. The distinction – as with this pair of stories – will often depend on the prejudices of the reader; one man's scare story is another's timely warning. Either way, their content has to satisfy something in the public appetite. These stories seem to me to offer circumstantial evidence of two things: that science, now more than ever, is widely and correctly assumed to get the public in a lather; and that the level of this anxiety is sufficient to tempt not only editors to report it, but pressure groups to exploit it.

I am not suggesting that anxiety about science is something new. Science is, of its nature, subversive. No other scheme for describing and explaining the world incorporates the means – indeed the necessity – of testing its own conclusions. All scientific 'truth' is provisional. A system that can and periodically does undermine even its own cherished certainties will never be easy to live with.

Neither am I claiming that science and its achievements have, of their nature, suddenly become more threatening just because we happen to be approaching the millennium. The progress of science takes little notice of the calendar. Indeed as the science writer Bernard Dixon has pointed out, suspicion of science and technology in the second half of this century was foreshadowed back in the opening years of the first half.

The novelist George Gissing wrote in 1903:

> I hate and fear science because of my conviction that, for long to come if not for ever, it will be the remorseless enemy of mankind. I see it destroying all simplicity and gentleness of life, all the beauty of the world; I see it restoring barbarism under the mask of civilisation; I see it darkening men's minds and hardening their hearts; I see it bringing a time of vast conflicts which will . . . whelm all the laborious advances of mankind in blood drenched chaos.

Strong stuff. Nearer to our own time we have Gordon Rattray Taylor's 1970 compendium of scientific and technological horrors, *The Doomsday Book*. By comparison with Gissing, the language is restrained. The prophecies, though, are not; the author's confident survey of chemical and radioactive pollution, overpopulation, resource depletion and much else was enough to leave even the most enthusiastic scientist wondering if the Stone Age might not after all have been the right place to call a halt to progress. And so it has gone on, with each decade producing a further crop of fears from biotechnology to holes in the ozone layer to global warming to shrinking willies. *Some* of the threats *may* have become more pressing – indeed I believe they have – but this hasn't all happened in the past few years.

So, if anxiety about science it not of itself a new development, and if the greater threats posed by science have not *suddenly* come into existence, what am I on about? *Is* there a millennial link? I am certain there is. But what's bringing our apprehensions about science ever closer to the boil at this particular time is predominantly a matter of perception: of heightened sensitivity. *Fin-de-siècle* fears and paranoias – swollen, at the end of this particular *siècle*, by the transition to a new *millénaire* (an event which can, perversely, unsettle even the toughest intellect) – are customary in every branch of human affairs. As we approach the year 2000, the impact of science and technology is already being felt as never previously, so it's hardly surprising that these things should become a point of attachment for the free-floating anxiety that always materialises in the run-up to this collective rite of passage.

The rational response to such anxiety is to remind oneself that all dating systems are arbitrary and that the year 2000 is also, to devout Jews, the far less intimidating 5760. Alas, it doesn't work. The millennium will not be denied. For good reasons or for bad, some areas of science and technology will soon be casting an even sharper and gloomier shadow. I am all for confronting anxieties about science; but let's remember, when we speak of *millennial* anxiety, that much of it is really no more than the calendar acting as a lens. Perhaps we should even offer thanks to the millennium for catalysing a scrutiny which needs to be undertaken, whatever the date.

In parallel with all the anxiety – perhaps contributing to it – there is a discernible public desire to *know* about science. The success of Stephen Hawking's *A Brief History of Time* is legendary. Surveys of what people claim to want on radio and television invariably reveal a demand for more science programmes. The bookstall sales of American news magazines are strongly influenced by their cover illustration, and when their editors first noticed that most years' best-selling issues included a disproportionate number featuring a science theme, they launched the glossy science magazine boom of the seventies. And yet, and yet . . . multitudes of Hawkings remain unopened on as many coffee tables; when the extra science programmes are broadcast, their ratings are seldom exceptional, and most of the new science titles produced by American magazine publishers survived a year or three, then sank.

The desire to understand science is real enough. So too is the feeling – especially about cosmology and particle physics – that there is knowledge to be acquired which can sharply alter the way the world looks. This is particularly so in the case of Stephen Hawking. Nobody can really doubt that part (and I only say 'part') of the success of that book is attributable to its author's own exceptional circumstances. Here is a brain which has not only survived betrayal by its body, but prospered – seemingly in inverse proportion. Everything about Hawking seems to hint at the possession of extraordinary insights. And here's the book, the product of that brain. Perhaps it will guide *us* towards those same insights! But somehow the urge to acquire them regularly fails to stay the course. In spite of the help provided by all the new books, programmes and magazine articles, science is still hard work and the mysteries often remain unpenetrated: a failure which, in itself, adds to the anxiety.

That people should harbour fears about the pace and direction of science and technology, and about some of their achievements, is understandable and reasonable. The rate of acquisition of knowledge has never been greater. Never have humans had to absorb so much, and update it so often. The time when facts acquired during secondary or even tertiary education could be counted on to serve for life has passed. Last decade's cutting edge is blunt by the time we enter this one; already in some areas it's last year's knowledge which is out of date.

Neither are the changes solely quantitative. Hitherto, most scientific – as opposed to philosophical or theological – enquiry has been directed at things outside ourselves: our physical environment and the laws governing the behaviour of matter; the plant and animal life surrounding us; the place of our planet in the solar system. When we began to study ourselves, we were first preoccupied with anatomy and physiology: safe, unthreatening topics. Now, though, science has turned inwards with a new determination. The realisation that besides comprehending heredity we shall soon be able to shape it has triggered ripples of uncertainty which are now aggregating into waves of something more like panic.

Even more irresistible as a research target is the brain. The most ambitious neurobiologists are intent on understanding the nature of consciousness. Achieving this goal would represent – to borrow from the historian Francis Fukuyama's description of the outcome of the Cold War - the end of biology. In the middle 1800s, Darwin's ideas challenged the role if not the existence of God, and so fostered doubts about religion; in the opening years of the next century, biology – by exploring the nature of the brain – will begin provoking anxiety about ourselves. How unsettling will it be for us to understand the neural mechanisms of love and hate and aesthetic appreciation and all the rest of those features of the mind by which we define ourselves? How shall we perceive them, and ourselves, when we have laid bare – or just laid – the ghost in the machine?

To personalise the matter, I like to think of myself as a hard-nosed rationalist, anxious to see dispelled the fog of neurobiological ignorance that prevents me from comprehending more than a fraction of my own fears, desires or motivations. All current explanations are wholly inadequate: those of the behaviourists strike me as simplistic; those of the analysts as absurdly fanciful or pleasantly poetic, but never to be taken literally. I have no religious belief, so this doesn't come into the picture. Confidently I claim I would welcome a better understanding of the workings of my own consciousness, and I also like to think that the prospect gives me no anxieties. But I say these things in the comfortable certainty that I will not actually have to face this knowledge for a decade or two – or perhaps ever in my own lifetime. The reality *might* leave me feeling rather different.

Genetics is as good a topic as any for fleshing out the bones of present and legitimate fear about the tangible achievements of science. As with most such advances, the public attitude is ambivalent: the presumed benefits are first acclaimed, if not hyped; then the drawbacks or abuses are revealed and demonised. Pre-natal diagnosis allows parents to find out if their unborn baby has one of an increasing number of inherited disorders, and creates the opportunity to terminate that pregnancy. How splendid, we say, to be able to prevent the birth of children whose lives are destined to be incomplete or potentially distressing. But the same procedure will identify the sex of the foetus, and allow parents for whom boy children are at a premium to abort females. How shameful, we protest, that a healthy infant should be destroyed simply because she's the wrong gender.

Some 4,000 human disorders are caused by defects in single genes. At present only a small minority can be detected by pre-natal testing, but the list for which tests have been developed lengthens by the month. Anyone who imagines that the ethical dilemmas of genetic testing begin and end with abortion is in for a shock. To test an adult for the Huntington's chorea gene, for example, is to find out if that individual is destined to face an early, unpreventable and unpleasant death; is such a test justified? Or again, many human illnesses are the product not of one gene but of several, each interacting with its fellows, and with the environment; if an unborn child has, say, a two-fold increase in his or her risk of dying early through heart disease, do you abort? Or do you reserve termination for the ten-fold baby? If you can identify the genes which predispose to slender and good-looking children, what do you do when testing casts up the probability that your own infant will be heavy and dull-witted? At what point does the comfortable expectation of a world with less inherited disease degenerate into a resurrection of the 1920s' and 30s' doomed infatuation with eugenics? That endeavour led to the Nazi gas chambers: a final solution devised to deal with a group of people already living. *New* final solutions, relying on elimination of the unwanted before they had achieved independent existence, would be less visible.

Some of the new technologies create scenarios that are not so much frightening as blackly comical. Frozen sperm already allow men to go on fathering children long after their death. Now, by transplanting the ovaries of an aborted foetus into an infertile woman, it will be possible to give birth to a child with the genes of a woman who has never lived!

The anxious questions pile up. What to do about insurance companies which demand to know the results of any genetic tests you may have had? How to respond to employers trying to shed employees whose genes reveal them to be more than averagely susceptible to the chemicals used in this or that industrial process? Requests which are reasonable from *their* point of view seem outrageously discriminatory from *yours*. The flow of questions and dilemmas will not abate. More likely the reverse, because the search for human genes has thus far been a fragmentary affair with laboratories choosing their targets at random. Now we have the Human Genome Project. Through this multi-million-dollar international scheme, research institutes around the world will collaborate to decode the entire human blueprint. Sooner or later it won't be simply a few selected chunks of DNA with which we'll be familiar; we'll know the lot.

'The philosophers have only interpreted the world in various ways,' wrote Karl Marx; 'the point is to change it.' He didn't have recombinant DNA technology in mind, but the quotation could serve as a motto for the worshipful company of genetic engineers. Having defined the nature of single gene defects, researchers have come up with manoeuvres for replacing them with copies of the good gene. The bigger challenge – and one which no researcher has yet had the hubris to tackle (or at any rate has admitted to tackling in a human) – is to alter the cells of the germ line. When the normal genes that would prevent cystic fibrosis are introduced into the lining of the respiratory tract, they expire with their host. But those same genes, introduced into cells destined to become eggs or sperm, would be carried forward to successive generations. We would be altering not just ourselves but our children, and our children's children. Only those burdened with a surfeit of confidence or a lack of imagination can fail to feel anxiety at such a prospect.

Genetics may be the current focus of concern about science but it's not alone. It's impossible here to list all the anxiogenic creations and by-products of science and technology, but a handful will indicate their number and diversity. Let's mention thalidomide, food irradiation, pesticide residues, global warming, nuclear power, nerve gas, H-bombs, brain-washing, *in vitro* fertilisation . . . but enough. You know the list as well as I. Some of these things are more real than others; some frighten only a few people, some frighten many; some certainly worry me. The point is that all of them can be *perceived* as a threat and, from the point of view of generating anxiety about what science and technology are up to, that is enough.

For all our increasing awareness of the *specific* achievements and consequences of science – frightening or otherwise – I suspect that the core of the reason why many people find it alienating and anxiety-provoking lies at an altogether deeper level. You could, to put it dramatically, say that science has dispensed with the use (not need) for God. For the past century or two, the scientific materialist view of the world has been briskly filling in the pit of incomprehension and uncertainty which, for most of man's history, could be filled *only* by religion. This is not the place to rehearse an old and familiar argument, so I must ask the reader to accept my view that there *is* a fundamental conflict between science and religion. The fact that many individuals – including scientists - subscribe to both is of no significance; cognitive dissonance is a feature of human psychology, and most of us find it possible to hold two opposed views at the same time.

I specified our *use* for God, not our *need*. If science were able to deal with incomprehension as satisfactorily as does religion, all would be well. One source of explanation, inspiration and solace would have replaced another; putting aside all nit-picking questions of objective truth, the human need for understanding would have been satisfied. But although I can frame my own comprehension of the world in terms of materialistic science, and find it intellectually and emotionally satisfying to do so, I am well aware that many people view this with distaste – or worse.

The philosopher Karl Popper has identified the appeal of religion as its claim to unfalsifiable certainty. In fact religion is not quite alone in staking out this ground; a handful of quasi-scientific theories – notably psychoanalysis and Marxism – have tried to establish a similar foothold. Bryan Magee, in his thankfully concise commentary on Popper, illustrates the essence of his subject's view of these and other such would-be sciences. 'Popper,'[1] writes Magee, 'often pointed out that the secret of the enormous psychological appeal of these various theories lay in their ability to explain everything. To know in advance that whatever happens you will be able to understand it gives you not only a sense of intellectual mastery but, even more important, an emotional sense of secure orientation in the world. Acceptance of one of these theories had, he observed, "the effect of an intellectual conversion or revelation, opening your eyes to a new truth hidden from those not yet initiated. Once your eyes were thus opened you saw confirming instances everywhere: the world was full of verifications of the theory. Whatever happened always confirmed it. Thus its truth appeared manifest; and unbelievers were people who clearly did not want to see the manifest truth; who refused to see it either because it was against their class interest, or because of their repressions which were still un-analysed and crying aloud for treatment."'

What comfort can science offer to compete with the soothing balm of an account of the world that explains everything? As the millennium approaches, how many will turn for reassurance to a system of knowledge which draws strict boundaries beyond which it refuses to venture; which, far from making claims for the infallibility of its insights, emphasises that each of them is provisional? This is not what we want to be told; this is not comforting.

Equally disconcerting to many is scientific reductionism. This necessary ingredient of science is sometimes portrayed as an egregious desire to strip bare all life-enhancing mystery and replace it with life-denying mechanical descriptions. By neglecting our yearning for something more than rational accounts of the world, and instead recognising nothing but the machine, science seems to be adding to our discomfort.

In at least one respect, you might think, science should be a source of comfort. To the extent that some of the fears we experience as we move towards the millennium stem from ignorance of the world around us, what better source of confidence could we hope for than science, and its pursuit of knowledge. But there is a further and perhaps even more intractable problem here: one created by the nature of scientific understanding. In his paradoxically titled book, *The Unnatural Nature of Science*, the biologist Lewis Wolpert argues persuasively that science does *not* rely on a 'natural' (commonsensical would be a reasonable synonym in this context) mode of thought.

To take the simplest of examples: it is reasonable, watching the sun rise in the east, cross the sky, and then set in the west, to suppose that this happens because it is circling the earth. The fallacy in this common sense explanation becomes apparent only when you know more about the true relationship of earth and sun. Or take the nature of white light. There is no *a priori* reason to suppose that this comprises light of many different wavelengths. Only through the empirical evidence of the spectrum formed when light is refracted by a raindrop or a prism does the truth become literally visible. And even then it is a truth which has little to do with common sense; things just are the way they are.

By the time you graduate to twentieth-century physics, common sense has dropped almost completely out of the frame. Relativity, black holes, quantum mechanics and the existence of more than three dimensions are not topics on which it is easy to hold a 'natural' conversation. To understand science is hard work, and getting harder. Even those areas – and there are many – which don't require the suspension of common sense aren't always accessible. To obtain pleasure and understanding from a contemporary novel it is not essential to have read Conrad, Dickens or Austen. It is certainly rewarding to know how English novels have developed; but this is an optional extra. By contrast, to pick up more than a superficial grasp of nuclear energy, you have to understand a fair amount about the fundamental physics of the atom. And a lot of science is like this: the upper levels of the edifice make sense only when you've dug down to look at the foundations. There's also the hurdle of terminology to be crossed. You cannot go very deep in either the life or the physical sciences before everyday words are no longer enough: much of the jargon of immunology, say, or of particle physics has no non-technical equivalent. The point is not that these obstacles can't be overcome; they can and are by thoughtful scientists and enthusiastic amateurs. But they aren't easily overcome. Many people lack the time, the skill, the motivation or the opportunity to make the required effort.

The likely consequence is that certain areas of science will become progressively less accessible to all but a tiny number of professionals, never mind to the general public. In the early nineteenth century, an educated man with time to spare – the celebrated 'gentleman scientist' – could reasonably hope to know most of what was available to be known of science. As the accumulation of knowledge accelerated, soon only professional scientists could make the claim. Then came the inevitable subdivision: only biologists knew what was happening in biology, physicists in physics, and so on. Nowadays, of course, biologists may have trouble keeping up just with their own (often narrowly circumscribed) branch of the subject. Some find the theory of relativity every bit as puzzling as non-scientists. But does this matter – not so much to science as to society?

I think it does, and I suspect it will fuel a great deal more anxiety about science and technology in the coming century. The optimist, of course, will argue that even if today's adults are a lost cause, changes in the content of education plus the adaptability of young minds will witness this or the next generation of children lapping up the most baffling ideas. As illustration they may point to the ease with which the average twelve-year-old masters a home computer. While fathers are still beating a pathway of near-despair through the manual, their children are already writing new software.

Well, maybe. While it is true that humans have been adapting for the past century and more to a world of increasing complexity, both in technology and in ideas, I am not sure that this process can continue indefinitely. By education and early career a scientist, and now – as for many years – by occupation a medical and science journalist, I should be ideally placed to cope with the pace of change. Time was when I did. But while I still relish an elegant piece of research or a new insight, I can't deny a tiny resentment about the ever more frequent need to keep on revising my knowledge – and do so with a brain which time does not make more flexible. It begins to make me feel slightly . . . anxious.

Some eight decades after Einstein published his general theory of relativity, how many people in Britain really understand it? Half a million? A quarter of a million . . . 50,000? I have no idea, but I would be surprised if the figure were much greater. The circumstances in which knowledge agreed to be special and important is confined to small groups of people is familiar in human societies. That phenomenon has generally been called religion, and the masters of the knowledge priests. Of course, there are fundamental differences between the bodies of learning called 'science' and 'religion', but the advent of a kind of scientific priesthood, in which a select group act as guardians of a body of wisdom too esoteric for the masses, is not beyond imagining. Herman Hesse envisaged something of the kind in his novel *The Glass Bead Game*, and some individuals whose knowledge and interests are remote from science might argue that we are there already. Either way, intellectual exclusion creates a state of continuous angst in which the urge to share understandings is perpetually frustrated by their incomprehensibility. Circumstances in which important knowledge is, for whatever reason, inaccessible to most members of a community generate instability. They are, ultimately, incompatible with democracy.

You may think this is all a bit exaggerated; to be frank, I am not entirely sure if I believe it myself. Although most of the panics turn out to be groundless (remember the 'polywater' scare in which a rogue molecule which had escaped from some laboratory was feared to be causing all the world's water to undergo polymerisation into something no doubt quite undrinkable) it's beyond dispute that the findings of science *are* sometimes of a kind which can be abused, and *do* therefore provide grounds for genuine anxiety. The new work on genetics is a case in point. I have few fears about the use of gene therapy applied to somatic cells; the scientists doing the work are well aware of the quite limited risks involved, and have a reassuring track record on safety. On the other hand, I would be extremely nervous of the consequences of a widespread and uncontrolled use of pre-natal sex determination. Its potential to cause social upheaval is inescapable, even if the extent of that upheaval must remain a matter of speculation.

In the end, though, what I most fear is not the abuse of science, but its rejection. Could such a thing – a partial reversal of the Enlightenment, no less – actually happen? The few examples we have are either so singular (the attempt by the Khmer Rouge to return Cambodia to 'Year Zero') or so narrowly eccentric (the US Bible Belt rejection of evolution in favour of creationism) that they illustrate nothing but themselves. On the whole, though, while I'd certainly be fearful if scientific rationalism were widely rejected, I don't believe it will be. We have mainlined on science and technology for too long, and become addicted. If for no other reason than that there are now so many of us on the planet, dreams of a widespread return to some pre-scientific agrarian existence are a distracting Utopian fantasy. Only a global catastrophe which destroyed technological civilisation could bring this about. (Though this, of course, is precisely what many people antagonistic to science believe it *is* doing. If it does happen, they will at least be able to say they told us so.)

What, then, is to be done? For responding to developments *falsely* perceived as a threat (and, yes, I am begging the question of who is to decide which are real and which imagined) I can suggest no remedy more effective than better public understanding. This is something which scientists themselves have realised as, belatedly, they take greater pains to explain their work to an increasingly distrustful populace. For real anxieties – genetic manipulation, the artificial prolongation of life, environmental pollution and all the rest of it – the remedy is vigilance and, whenever these things threaten us, or diminish us, or are done for no reason other than that they *can* be done, protest. *Selective* protest. Railing against science as a whole will achieve nothing. This genie, as I've said, will not be forced back into its lamp.

Do not, let me add, rely on the ethics of the scientists themselves to shield you from anxiety. Although most of them agree on certain codes of conduct – not falsifying results, sharing information wherever possible, not stealing others' data and so on – they have no generally accepted ethical code. Scientific pressure groups sometimes try to persuade their fellow workers not to pursue certain controversial topics or accept research grants from 'tainted' sources, but that's about as far as it goes. I'm no longer convinced that the stock response to this state of affairs – that scientists as a group have certain social responsibilities, and should act accordingly – is the right one. As a keen, twenty-something tyro researcher, I went to meetings of the (now defunct) British Society for Social Responsibility in Science, and bewailed what seemed to me the social indifference of my peers. I still believe that individual scientists should act within their own consciences. But over-reliance on organisational self-policing would be a dangerous stratagem. What the scientists might believe to be important or satisfactory would not necessarily accord with the wishes of society at large. If the control of science *were* ever to be governed by the conscience of the scientists, *they* might start to feel it's their right to lay down the law to *you* on what's acceptable and what's not. Better by far that individual scientists should be free to pursue their interests, and then justify that freedom by making themselves publicly accountable.

An anxiety even less easily overcome is the alienated, dispossessed state of mind which science will increasingly induce in those who do not feel themselves to be part of it. But maybe science itself – scientific medicine – can offer a remedy. Not a pharmacological one; neither mass anxiolysis (the Valium Retreat) nor mass euphoria (the Prozac Escape) are even remotely attractive. But psychology and psychiatry have devised more direct ways of trying to refashion inappropriate or disadvantaging states of mind. 'Flooding' is a form of behaviour therapy in which subjects are forced to confront the irrational components of what may be otherwise reasonable anxieties until they learn to cope with them. It is sometimes painful; but with spiders, heights, flying and other such sources of acute anxiety it has a reasonably good track record. The point of the therapy is not to render subjects *totally* fearless (black widows, unfenced cliffs and poorly maintained aircraft *should* be feared), but to neutralise anxieties that are excessive or counterproductive. Public attitudes towards science are bedevilled by both. So could a therapeutic confrontation help to overcome them? An example may help to answer the question. Imagine a man to whom a life worth living is one with an external purpose and goal set by a benign creator. By such beliefs he keeps his anxiety in check. What alternative can science offer him? A machine model of human beings who have no creator, for whom death is final, and whose only purposes are *self*-created? Not promising. The question is: can he find within science something more satisfying than he might have expected? I think that he – all of us – can.

I would propose an absurdly fanciful, but pleasantly cheap experiment. Our man would be locked (voluntarily, of course) in a room with a computer screen running an evolutionary simulation devised by Dan Nilsson and Susanne Pelger of Lund University, and intended by them to demonstrate the prodigious capacity of living systems to advance their own development. I think it can be deployed to do more than that: to refute the view that a scientific perspective must be emotionally bleak and spiritually stultifying.

Nilsson and Pelger[2] wanted to simulate the evolution of a simple, camera-type of eye. Their model had to deal with one of the standard objections to evolution by natural selection: that while a fully formed and working eye is beneficial to its owner, and therefore confers a selective advantage, a half-formed and non-functional eye offers *no* benefits and therefore *no* selective advantage. Can natural selection really perfect something which, until it has reached an advanced stage of development, seems to have no adaptive value? As their starting point the two researchers chose a primitive light receptor: a flat patch of skin comprising a sheet of light-sensitive cells sandwiched between an outer, protective and transparent layer and an inner, darkly pigmented one. As would happen naturally in successive generations of a real organism, Nilsson and Pelger allowed their model to deform itself at random, but within fixed limits. Playing the part of Nature red in tooth and claw, they programmed the computer to select only those of the random changes that improved the 'fitness' of the system as a useful seeing device.

Let our volunteer press the start button, and watch the screen. What he'll see is an image which twists and turns, folding and bending this way and that. Step by step – unscripted, unrehearsed, and with no pre-ordained goal – the patch of light-sensitive cells modelled within the computer will turn itself into a perfectly 'designed' eye.

I find this experiment not only appealing but exhilarating. As our man sits there at the computer, watching while an electronic device following a handful of simple rules allows something as intricate as an eye to create itself there on the screen in front of him, will it be anxiety he'll feel? Surely not. Amazement, maybe. Perhaps, disbelief. But if he can make the mental leap from computer screen to real life, he might – and here I admit I am being optimistic – he might begin to sense the wonderment which science has to offer the receptive mind.

The comforts of science are, admittedly, unsentimental: on the Spartan side, you might say. But they are also magnificent. In telling us that the most exquisitely complicated forms of life, including ourselves, are the product not of a creator, but of self-creation, they confer the dignity that comes with knowing we are beholden to nothing and to no one but ourselves. More than that, they offer us the chance to experience awe: a sensation powerful enough to swamp any amount of anxiety. The simple experiment with the eye – a parable, if you like – demonstrates that science can generate awe as effectively as religion, and that knowledge can be life-enhancing as well as unsettling.

Science – whether viewed as a particular set of facts and theories or, more correctly, as a way of acquiring knowledge about the world – will not go away. No use pining for the advent of a New Age full of mystic auras and magic crystals. When the warm starry night above Glastonbury turns into an ordinary chilly English dawn, it's science, not superstition, which is still there. Yes, science *is* tough-minded about the world, and often *does* create anxiety. Like any human activity which can be harmful as well as beneficial, it needs to be controlled. Coping with the anxiety provoked by what science reveals of the nature of our existence will not be easy. But, given the right mindset, science itself can also provide some of the antidotes.

Finally, if the going gets *really* anxious, first recall and then try to believe the words of the painter Georges Braque: 'L'Art est fait pour troubles. La Science réassure.[3]

Notes

1 Bryan Magee, *Popper* (1973) published by Fontana/Collins.
2 'A pessimistic estimate of the time required for an eye to evolve'. Proceedings of the Royal Society of London (1994), **256**, 53-58.
3 *Day and Night: notebooks* (1952).

Bidisha Bandyopadhyay

Young and Anxious

When I was very young, there was nothing to be anxious about. Nothing could perturb me: the world's troubles could have piled up on my doorstep and I would not have noticed, understood or cared. For the first six years of my life, I lived with my parents in what is now considered a 'bad' area of London. Those years were what I now consider to be the ultimate in decadence and hedonism. I remember shopping with my father, trips to the park with my mother, endless birthday parties and group outings. As an only child, I spent a lot of time daydreaming. I didn't seem to be able to understand the difference between fantasy and reality, waking from vivid dreams believing my nocturnal adventures had actually occurred. One hour I would be flying several feet above the ground or able to breathe underwater; another, I was being pushed against the wall of the playground by a group of older kids demanding, 'Do you speak English? Why is your face like that? Aren't you meant to have an earring in your nose?'

In the same way that I could not distinguish between dreams and real life, I had no concept of time passing. I recall, on New Year's Eve in 1984, when I was six years old asking my mother, 'What happens after eighty-four?'

'Well, eighty-five.'

'Why do the numbers change?'

'Because another year's passed.'

From 1978 to 1989 every year was ended by a six-week trip to India. My grandparents lived in a large house in Calcutta, and every time I visited them I sensed I was moving further away from the type of life I witnessed there. The first language I'd spoken had actually been Bengali, picked up from hearing my parents speak to each other. But then I was taught English, and as the years went on I found it increasingly difficult to slip into my native tongue in India. It now bears the stilted mark of a foreigner.

While I returned to my schoolfriends every September, Calcutta rotted. Corruption in the government and civil service worsened; the gap between rich and poor continued to widen; the number of starving children and deformed ancients lining the road and bazaars grew. Contorted and diluted Western trends reached the Asian youth.

Although I found my links with India enriching, I resented any efforts to maintain a sham sense of Indian 'culture' and community spirit when there was no emotional compulsion behind it. Having thus rejected my racial duties, I grew up in a kind of cultural limbo – bilingual, undeniably Asian in appearance, an atheist, considered an outsider by the British, and also by the Indian.

The mid-eighties are memorable to me only as the beginning of a seemingly interminable cycle of education and school holidays. As a generation we naturally had no sense of ourselves as part of a society yet; our only community was contained within the walls of our homes. We could not really experience the mood of confidence in economic and business practices, the cross-Atlantic right-wing revolution, explosion of consumerism, the impact of feminism or the discovery of AIDS.

By the end of the eighties what did develop for the first time in us was a kind of despondency, a questioning of what we saw around us. The nineties marked the beginning of my generation's adolescence, a time when we naturally tried to find and assert our identity. We were told by magazines and newspapers to expect ten years of calm, reason and tranquillity. But the years passed, and the decade reflected no decisive shift in the national lifestyle or attitude. Health food shops and producers of cruelty-free cosmetics cashed in on the guilt-boom after the ruthlessness of the eighties, but no fundamental changes occurred. In the grip of a recession, becoming tired after years of Conservative government, it seemed as if people were seeking some rest and consolation after the hysteria of the previous decade. There was a sense that anything people had previously put their faith in – religion, politics, the family – had been exposed as corrupt or meaningless.

The adults' depression of the last ten years or so has resulted in a general sense of youthful nihilism. We have a need to discover new territory, to create our own moral and social code. This is most noticeable in the arts: the films of Quentin Tarantino, the art of Damien Hirst, the clothes of Gaultier have all typified the decade's need for extreme drama and dramatic statement. To an older generation of people growing up in the post-Second World War period, the nineties would seem like the worst science fiction film:

full of crumbling institutions, injustice, poverty, dangerous drugs, dangerous sex, violence and disease.

Although it might seem improbable, the attitude of the young to increasing violence in the world is complacent. It is undeniable that the films, art and books of today are full of violent characters and events. Some people might argue that this approach is a healthy one: we become aware of the darker compulsions in human nature and see what damage they can do; others argue that people may find the violence glamorous or provocative. To today's young the violence in art is, admittedly, attractive. Perhaps because many of us have had stable, secure backgrounds we find suicidal, homicidal or psychotic characters and deeds intriguing; we follow stories of rapes, killings and attacks in the media with macabre enthusiasm. None the less, any young person (especially female) who has felt scared walking or travelling alone at night, or in a 'rough' area, will know that even the most petty violence is far more sordid than any film. But each individual, while being aware of violence and possibly even fascinated by it, harbours the belief that they will not come into personal contact with it. This attitude is not a result of any modern state of mind, but something relating to youth's timeless naivete: we always believe ourselves personally exempt from harm and because we feel we are basically 'safe', we can be told of rising figures of all types of violence without experiencing any personal fear, and without it affecting our thirst for the extreme.

It could also be argued that our acceptance of violence as a part of modern life is related to a feeling of powerlessness: we are citizens of a state that gives us no real authority so, perversely, we allow violence to escalate because we feel we can do nothing to stop it. It is fair to say, however, that many young people have never questioned this assumed powerlessness. We have never really tested the country's political institutions, but have imperceptibly absorbed our parents' misanthropic attitude.

The way politics is presented to us has reinforced our impression that what goes on at Westminster has little effect on our lives. In schools, politics is taught text-book style: the Civil Service, House of Lords and the welfare system are examined and observed as a scientist would the carcass of a long-dead animal. We seem to have inherited from our parents, reinforced by the fact that none of us has experienced a Labour government, political apathy and passivity. The political system is regarded by them (and, to a certain extent, by us as well) as a son who's gone irrevocably astray.

Contrary to what one might expect of the hot-blooded ranks of youth in today's society, we don't care much for politics. It must be said that if I weren't a student of politics, and was left to try and decipher newspapers unaided, I would not be able to understand half of what goes on in British government. Although as idealistic juveniles we may claim to want justice and happiness for all, in truth it is only the hip, fashionable issues of the day that can incite more than a cynically raised eyebrow. Of course, we worry about the economy and employment prospects for the future, yet these problems are so enormous we cannot contemplate any possible revolution in national fortunes: we do not kid ourselves – the future looks bad. Issues such as the decriminalisation of cannabis, the Criminal Justice Act, personal identification and tagging, laws on immigration, general civil rights and changes in the gay age of consent are attractive to us because they give us a chance to make some noise defending the three governing principles of being young: freedom, individuality and good times. Even so, most of the 'young' people we see on TV opposing, for example, attempted urbanisation of rural areas are in their early to mid twenties.

Nonetheless, even we feel that the political process has reached a critical time: whereas our twenty-something siblings have probably never bothered to vote, the coming generation, voting for the first time in 1997, may feel it can tip the balance. Politics in the future, then, can go one of many ways. If the Conservative Party wins the election, we might not be able to overcome our political anaesthesia; if the Labour Party wins, and we see palpable improvements in the way the country's run, some of our faith in Parliament might be restored; if Labour wins and we see no change, politics will have finally achieved the farcical status we had always suspected it was capable of.

Young people are essentially selfish, and it is really problems related to our personal futures, our personal identities and our personal careers that concern us most, rather than petty externals such as politics or violence. Although we may share in a general pessimism we still, perhaps without customary naivety, have ambitions and hopes for success in the future. However, many people believe that collective action and aspiration don't work: racially, we will might not be willing to show fealty to people in our 'ethnic community' simply because we share the same skin tone; sexually, the notion of 'sisterhood' has been an unrealistic one, and strong female role models are a better idea. The idea of collective action is unrealistic: shared ambitions, not human love, are what holds people together in these situations, but those ambitions have become confused, too diverse, contradictory or unrealistic. The alternative view might seem like a typical Tory attitude: each person for themself, climbing the ladder and stepping over other people in the process. But this is the reality: it is the only method left, and, in a world so full of noise and confusion, the fittest want their survival instincts to be recognised.

Maybe we as a generation are simply being pragmatic rather than idealistic; we have learned to forge our own version of old ideas. Feminism is an example of this. As we entered our teens at the beginning of the nineties, we knew roughly what feminism was: the struggle of women to attain social equality with men – equal pay, equal rights, equal roles. As such, we were all feminists: career orientated, self-confident and ambitious. Yet we were not entirely comfortable with the f-word.

For us feminism required its own generational revolution. We would not feel content as barren automatons setting our sights on professional supremacy only, neither would we want to prove our inner strength by being able to juggle work, romance and family. We don't even want to think about kids, jobs and life-partners. Youth means experimentation, fun and opportunity. The type of feminism we, as young, clever, free, beautiful females want is a much more realistic, modern one which does not deny our interest in life's less cerebral aspects. Teenagers are obsessed with sex: one thing that defines teenaged social events is the meat-trading aspect. Camille Paglia's *Sexual Personae* is the only book I have read which understands this most basic element of what it is to be young and female:

> Sexuality is a murky realm of contradictions and ambivalence . . . Eroticism is mystique, the aura of emotion and imagination around sex. It cannot be 'fixed' by codes of social or moral convention.

We want feminism in the next century to allow us a certain degree of freedom and enjoyment without the stigma (surely outmoded now?) of cheapness, fastness, wantonness or looseness. We are perfectly capable, and more than willing, to confess ourselves feminists and yet be sexually aggressive, predatory and uninhibited. We will, of course, be accused of using masculine tactics in a game of social supremacy, but I would say that rather than adopting male patterns of behaviour, we would merely be reclaiming the patterns of natural human behaviour which have been forced out of us. We need to be able, within the undeniably feminist context of advancing the identity, status and strength of women, to show that we can separate the emotional from the physical and become, to quote Camille Paglia again, 'self-exalting females of cold male will, with subtle sexual ambiguities of manner and look'.

It seems that every area of life is under attack: even the sexual freedom of young people has been checked by the very real threat of AIDS. Hopefully, my generation will be the first of many who practise safe sex. We only dimly remember the panic when AIDS was discovered in the eighties, neither do any of us share the ignorant view that it is an exclusively homosexual illness, or that it can be transmitted via kissing, toilet seats or sharing a glass, etc. Instead, every message we receive about sex is immediately followed with a reminder that the only type of satisfying sexual behaviour is *safe* sexual behaviour. Because the tragedy is so great, and because we know that we can prevent it becoming worse, those of my age (who, at sixteen or seventeen could almost be forgiven for immaturity and stupid behaviour) are taking responsibility for their own bodies, and in that way also caring about the welfare of other people. For once, young people have listened to what grown-ups are telling them: it is generally seen as clever, fashionable, socially-aware and perfectly acceptable to practise safe sex.

Around the same time that the shock of AIDS meant people had to reassess and redefine their sexual behaviour, the nightlives of young people were being altered radically by drugs. Ecstasy and Microdots (both forms of MDMA), acid and speed became regular 'recreational' drugs – they were taken at raves every weekend by youngsters who otherwise led perfectly normal, toxin-free lives.

As with violence, drug-taking is seen as extreme, transcendental, cool, glamorous, slightly risky. Modern culture has embraced sex and violence, and drugs complete the triumvirate: John Travolta shooting up in the film *Pulp Fiction* made heroin seem like a fantastic and desirable experience, while part of the notoriety of the writer Will Self is due to his well-documented abuse of hard drugs. The suicide of Nirvana's singer and junkie Kurt Cobain in 1994 became one of the decade's most beautiful events.

Es, trips and dope are, for middle-class kids at least, extremely cheap and very easy to get hold of direct from dealers or friends-of-friends. I know of at least five prominent private schools in London where boys and girls in the sixth form sell drugs (at a large profit) to children in lower years.

At the moment, only a few younger clubbers are taking any notice of the increasing number of drug-related disaster stories. In the last year or so, we have been hearing more and more about people who have been to clubs on a regular Saturday night, have taken their customary ecstasy tab, and have fallen extremely ill or died either because of overheating due to artificially increased metabolism and fervent dancing, or from over-consumption of liquid (ironically, to combat the overheating caused by the tab). We have always found risk attractive, and it is our wont to try and cause ourselves a certain amount of damage; as with violence, we never really believe something terrible will happen to us. The thrill of illicit palliatives will always be tempting to the young; the death-toll will have to reach AIDS-proportions before you see any change in our attitudes and practices. In fact, the general sense of pessimism these days might influence us further – with both the availability of drugs and the spending power of middle-class teenagers increasing dramatically, we could turn to coke and smack on a more permanent basis for solace from a cruel world.

The contradictions in our attitudes towards drugs are applicable to all aspects of young people's lives. There will always be an awareness of risk, and also a temptation to court danger. Although we might share some of our parents' fears, we wish to be free of outmoded attitudes. Our role – as any young generation's must be – is to discover the new anxieties of the age and, through trying to combat them, establish a new outlook.

The future may not look encouraging. Racially, socially, culturally, we are in the process of revising codes of behaviour, redefining attitudes and confronting modern dilemmas. Continual disappointment has led to politics being considered more of a national pantomime, part-comedy and part-tragedy, than a tool of the people. Unemployment figures show that we can no longer lose ourselves in work, nor, judging by divorce rates, can we escape into married bliss. One would be forgiven for thinking that my generation has been polluted by the prevalent universal cynicism and mood of dislocation. Yet still, people have an innate belief in their ability to change things. Any problem is seen as a challenge, any obstacle merely a test of strength. The next century can only be regarded as one more opportunity for us to try and effect some good. We, as Thomas Hardy put it in *Tess of the d'Urbervilles* over a hundred years ago, are full of 'unexpended youth bringing with it hope, and the invincible instinct towards self-delight.'

Notes on Contributors

Sarah Dunant is a writer and broadcaster, whose television work included presenting BBC2's cultural magazine The Late Show for a number of years. She is editor of *The War of the Words* (Virago, 1994) and seven novels including *Snow Storms in a Hot Climate* (Virago, 1995) and *Transgressions* (Virago, 1997).

Roy Porter is professor in the social history of medicine at the Wellcome Institute for the History of Medicine. He is currently working on a general history of medicine, on the history of Bethlem Hospital and on the Enlightenment in Britain. Recent books include *Doctor of Society: Thomas Beddoes and the Sick Trade in Enlightenment England* (Routledge, 1991) and *London: A Social History* (Hamish Hamilton, 1994).

Linda Grant is an author and journalist. Her first novel, *The Cast Iron Shore*, was published in 1996. She is a feature writer on the *Guardian*.

Geoff Mulgan is director of Demos, a visiting professor at University College, London, and author of *Communication and Control: networks and the new economies of communication* (Polity Press, 1991).

Mary Midgley was formerly senior lecturer in philosophy at the University of Newcastle-upon-Tyne. Her books include *Beast & Man*, *Wickedness*, *Science as Salvation* and *The Ethical Primate*.

The late **Oscar Moore** was editor-in-chief of Screen International, and a regular contributor to the *Guardian*, for whom he wrote a column about living with AIDS. Moore's first novel, *A Matter of Life and Sex*, was published in 1990, and *PWA*, a collection of his columns, was published after his death which was in September 1996.

Michael Ignatieff is a historian and writer, currently completing a biography of the liberal philosopher, Isaiah Berlin.

Michael Neve is a university teacher whose subjects include the history of psychiatry and the life sciences. He has edited the work of Charles Darwin and William Hazlitt.

Fred D'Aguiar is the author of three books of poems and two novels, most recently the novel *Dear Future* and the forthcoming *Bill of Rights*, a book-length poem (both from Chatto & Windus).

Susie Orbach is a psychotherapist and writer. In 1976 she co-founded The Women's Therapy Centre in London and in 1981 The Women's Therapy Centre Institute in New

York. Her bestselling first book *Fat is a Feminist Issue* (1978) continues to be hugely influential. Since 1991 she has written the only regular psychoanalytic newspaper column in the western world. She lives in London with her partner and their two children.

Geoff Watts read zoology before drifting into medical research. Having acquired a PhD, but lost the urge to do research, he reasoned the best way of escaping the laboratory while staying in touch with science and medicine was to write about them. He was deputy editor of *World Medicine* magazine and now presents Radio 4's Medicine Now.

Bidisha Bandyopadhyay was born in London in 1978, so will be twenty-one in the year 2000. Her first novel *Seahorses* was published in 1997. She studies English at Oxford University.